SUMMER OF CHANGE

The Springs—One

ELENA AITKEN

Also by Elena Aitken

The Springs Series

Summer of Change

Falling Into Forever

Second Glances

Winter's Burn

Midnight Springs

She's Making A List

Summit of Desire

Summit of Seduction

Summit of Passion

Fighting For Forever

The Springs Collection: Volume 1

The Springs Collection: Volume 2

The Springs Collection: Volume 3

The Springs Complete Collection - Books 1-10

The McCormicks

Love in the Moment

Only for a Moment

One more Moment

In this Moment

From this Moment

Our Perfect Moment

Destination Paradise

Shelter by the Sea

Escape to the Sun

Hidden in the Sand

Ever After

Choosing Happily Ever After

Needing Happily Ever After

Wanting Happily Ever After

Fighting Happily Ever After

We Wish You A Happily Ever After

Keeping Happily Ever After

Finding Happily Ever After

Seeking Happily Ever After

Cherishing Happily Ever After

Ever After: Volume One (Books 1-4)

Stand Alone Stories

All We Never Knew

Drawing Free

Sugar Crash

Composing Myself

Betty & Veronica

The Escape Collection

Vegas

Nothing Stays in Vegas

Return to Vegas

His to Tame

His to Seek

Hers for the Season

Bears of Grizzly Ridge: Books 1-4

Bears of Grizzly Ridge: Books 5-8

Halfway Series

Halfway to Nowhere

Halfway in Between

Halfway to Christmas

Chapter One

TRENT HARRISON SHUFFLED the ever-growing stack of papers on his desk and resisted the urge to shove them all to the floor. Sure, it would feel good on some level to watch them all flutter to the ground where he could kick them out of sight. A clean desk, if even for a moment, would almost be worth the fallout, but what would be the point? The work wasn't going away.

With a sigh, Trent dropped into his chair and picked up the paper on the top of the stack. He couldn't ignore the messages, especially because he knew exactly who they were from. The Springs, the resort he'd been working on and developing for years, was finally only weeks away from opening. They simply needed to put the final touches on everything and his dream would finally be realized. But along with the opening came the inevitable panic from the investors. Their top investors, the Braxtons, were already breathing down their necks to get reservations up and make sure they had the rooms full on opening. These things took time and although Trent wasn't the least bit worried, that wasn't what the investors wanted to hear.

Trent would make it happen. The Braxtons—more specifi-cally the younger Braxton, Les—didn't have anything to worry about. If there was one thing Trent Harrison and his partner and brother, Dylan, knew, it was the hotel business. The Springs had been their dream for years. And after everything they'd gone through to make that dream a reality, the last thing they were going to do was let it fail. Now all he had to do was convince his investors of that.

He scanned the memo. Just as he'd thought. Les had called again, demanding an update on the latest numbers. If only he could deal primarily with Samuel Braxton, the patriarch of the family. But no, it seemed like father had put son in charge of this particular investment. And now Les, and his need to please his father, had become Trent's problem.

"Dammit," Trent said to the empty room. "Just back off."

"Sorry, I didn't mean to intrude." Carmen Kincaid, manager of guest relations and his brother's girlfriend, walked through the door, her hands up in front of her.

"Not you, Carmen."

"I figured as much." Carmen smiled, and Trent tried to let himself feel better. His brother's girlfriend was one of the warmest, sincerest women he'd ever met. Not to mention beau-tiful. Plus it was a miracle she still spoke to him, let alone considered him a friend, after the way he'd almost sabotaged her relationship with Dylan months ago. He'd since learnt to keep his skepticism regarding relationships to himself.

"What has you yelling at your empty office?" She perched in a chair across from him.

He waved a hand in the air and shoved the offending message away. "It's nothing." Trent ignored the raised eyebrow Carmen gave him. "To what do I owe the pleasure of your visit this afternoon?"

She gave him a knowing smile. It wasn't a secret that Dylan

told Carmen everything. Really, it was kind of like having two partners. Not that Trent minded. Not really. He liked Carmen, and he trusted her. He just didn't trust the relationship. Or any relationship, for that matter. If he could place his bets, he'd bet against it lasting.

"Dylan and I were talking about how to raise awareness of the Springs and I had an idea to bring in what could be some exclusive business," she said.

"I'm listening." He leaned his elbows on his desk. If anyone would have an idea to boost business, it would be Carmen. She was the best there was, which was part of the reason he'd wanted to take her from Castle Mountain Lodge, the resort he'd worked at previously. The fact that she'd fallen in love with his brother and come to the Springs on her own, just made that a little easier.

Carmen pulled her chair closer and dropped the folder she was clutching on the desk. She swiped her long dark hair behind her shoulder and flipped the file open with a flourish. "When we were creating the brand for the Springs, we talked a lot about the healing properties of the waters here, right?" Trent nodded. The natural hot springs were the entire reason for constructing the resort. "And," Carmen continued, "we created an entire marketing plan around attracting people here so they could heal themselves, right?" Trent nodded again. "All our marketing materials focus on healing the body from what ails them. But what we only barely touch on is healing the mind."

Trent leaned back in his chair and crossed his leg over his knee. He knew what she was going to say. Carmen had talked him into adding yoga and meditation to the list of services, despite his skepticism, but he didn't like where she was going with this particular train of thought.

"Don't worry," she said. "I'm not going to try to convince

you to take a yoga class to calm your mind. I've pretty much given up on that." She rolled her eyes, but her smile gave her away. "I know you don't believe in all that stuff."

"It's not that I don't believe."

"You just don't see the value."

"Not for me." A wry smile played on his lips. "But if our guests want it and are willing to pay for it, that's reason enough for me."

"And I get that." She nodded. "But maybe you could personally see some value in stilling the mind." She shot him a look. Trent merely shrugged in return.

He'd hear her out, but only because he respected and liked Carmen. And she was probably right about it all being good for business.

"Anyway," she continued. "I think we should take the theme of healing a step further. Why not offer a special weekend that's focused on healing relationships?"

"Relationships?"

The last thing Trent wanted to talk about was relationships. Or his lack thereof. Carmen could add that to the list of things he didn't believe in and wanted nothing to do with. Especially if it was going to be the focus of his resort.

"Exactly," Carmen said, unaware of his internal protests. She pulled a sheet of paper from the folder and held it out to him. Instead of taking it, he glanced down on what looked like copy for a couples retreat advertisement. She shook the paper, but when he still didn't take it, she dropped it in front of him, letting it flutter to his desk. "We'll offer an all-inclusive weekend for couples who need to reconnect or heal their rela-tionship. We can have expert therapists come in—"

"Therapists? We have those."

"No. We have physical therapists. I'm talking about rela-tionship therapists. And only the best. We'll also have activities like couples massages and romantic picnics. Of course, we already have the finest chefs. And if we offer room service and—"

"Stop." Trent held up his hand, warding off any more cutesy couple ideas. "This is not the Lodge."

Carmen's face fell. She'd been the customer service manager at Castle Mountain Lodge, which was known for its romantic ambience, for years and she'd been working hard to create something different at the Springs. It was a sore spot for both of them, and Trent knew it.

"I know that, Trent," she said through gritted teeth. "But it's not a romantic escape we're offering; it's a healing and therapeutic weekend."

"I don't see it like that." He purposely took a file from the stack on his desk and put it on top of the advertisement. "It's not happening." He pretended to be engrossed in whatever it was that was written on the memo in front of him. Maybe she'd get the message and leave him alone. The idea of being surrounded by people in love was enough to make him go out in search of a woman who was interested in a commitment of exactly one night. Something he hadn't let himself indulge in since moving to the town of Cedar Springs. He'd been too busy working. But now that the idea had taken—

"Really?" Carmen pushed her chair back, making a scratching sound on the tile floor that made Trent's skin crawl and his attention snap back to the woman in front of him. "It's a damned good idea, Trent. And I don't see you with a better one."

It was a good idea, not that Trent was about to tell her that. But the last thing he wanted was a hotel full of couples prancing about. As if it wasn't bad enough to have Dylan and Carmen flaunting themselves in front of him. They were both setting themselves up for disappointment when it inevitably didn't work out. Trent met her eyes, and shrugged. "I'm not worried. The doors aren't even open yet, and we're starting to book up. It's not going to be an issue."

Carmen dropped her arms in exasperation. "Trent." She waited for him to look up at her. "At least consider it."

"Okay," he agreed. "I'll consider it." Her face split into a smile, so he didn't think it was the perfect time to tell her he didn't plan on reconsidering the idea any time soon. "Is there anything else?"

"Yes." Her eyes narrowed and Trent had the distinct feeling he wasn't going to like what she had to say next. "When was the last time you got out of here?"

"Pardon?"

"Away from the Springs. When was the last time you went down to town?"

He shrugged. Had she read his mind about needing some female companionship of his own?

"That's what I thought. You need to go."

Trent sighed, trying unsuccessfully to mask his growing irritation. "Why?"

"I think it's a good idea for us to do something good for the town," Carmen said.

So, not just to get laid? he thought and tried to focus on her words.

"To build goodwill between the locals and the resort," she continued. "Maybe we could have an open house night for everyone with food and drinks, and offer tours of the resort. Maybe we could even open the pools up for—"

"Whoa. You want to open it up?"

She shrugged. "Maybe not. It was just an idea. Maybe there's something else we could do. Just to let the people of Cedar Springs know that we're friends, not enemies."

"Why would we be…" He didn't bother finishing the

thought because he already knew not everyone in town was thrilled about the opening of the resort. Despite the fact that they were providing jobs and bringing more tourism to the area, there were definitely a group of locals who saw them as outsiders. Enemies. He shrugged. "It's actually a pretty good idea." And maybe while he was there…

Carmen laughed. "And that's why you hired me." She winked at him before he could say different, and turned to leave. "Oh, and while you're down there," she paused and reached up to her hair, "get yourself a haircut. You're looking a bit scruffy, boss."

She slipped from the room before Trent could say another word. Trent smiled and shook his head. As infuriating as she could be, Carmen meant well and she really did care. Even if her presence with his brother reminded him on a daily basis of what he didn't have.

What he'd had and let go. But it almost cost him everything once. And he wasn't going to make that mistake again. Especially not when everything was on the line. No, the Springs was too important. He pushed away from his desk and wandered over to the window. When the Harrison brothers designed their offices, they both made sure they had huge windows so that even if they spent their days making sure the Springs was successful, at least they'd have the view to get them through. After all the years he'd spent working at the Lodge, Trent had grown used to being in the mountains. Although Cedar Springs was a few hours away, the mountains were the same and that brought a least a little bit of comfort, Trent thought, even if it was the only thing that felt familiar these days.

Suck it up, man. He would have slapped himself if he could have. Trent was not the type of man to waste even a second of energy on feeling sorry for himself or things he couldn't control. The fact was, he could control the Springs.

And he'd worked too damn hard to let it slip through his fingers.

Carmen was right; they should do something nice for the people of Cedar Springs. After all, he planned to make it home for a long time to come. He ran a hand through his hair and tugged at the roots. Carmen was right, again; he was in desperate need of a haircut. It was much shaggier than he liked to wear it, but with everything he'd had going on, there hadn't been time. He took one more look out the window before he turned and straightened his suit. But there was no time like the present. Besides, whatever he would find in town was bound to be a whole lot more interesting than calling Les Braxton.

THE SUN WAS SHINING high overhead by the time Samantha Burke finished up with Lorne Walton, her account manager at the bank. She lifted her face to the warm sun, and tried to calm down before heading back to her bar, the Grizzly Paw. After all, it wasn't Lorne's fault he couldn't approve her loan. She knew she wasn't a good credit risk. Not after having to throw everything she had into buying the bar from her father. But it was Lorne's fault that he was such a jerk about it.

She swallowed hard, remembering the way he'd lectured her on trying to run a business in a small town and how the Grizzly Paw was going to be at risk of going under if something didn't give. Sam kicked at a stone on the sidewalk. She knew exactly what it was, too. The stupid resort that was going in up the road. It was changing the fabric of her town. People were scared, nervous about how the Springs opening would change the dynamic of their town. They were staying home, not eating out at the Paw anymore.

She took a minute to look around the main street of her beloved small town. In the green at the end of the street, kids played while their mothers chatted over coffee at one of the picnic tables. Sam could walk down to the lake, and on her way she'd be greeted by name by everyone she passed. The people of Cedar Springs were close. They looked out for one another and they cared about their picturesque mountain town. Outsiders weren't going to care. They were going to travel into town and destroy the peace and quiet, not to mention the extra cars, noise, and garbage they were likely to bring with them.

She sighed and laughed at herself a little because she knew if anyone could hear her thoughts, she'd be accused of being a crotchety old woman. And it wasn't that; she just wanted what was best. And as far as she could tell, it wasn't the Springs hotel.

With a shake of her head, she squeezed her files tight to her chest and walked back to the bar at the end of the road.

"Excuse me?" A deep male voice stopped her. "Can I ask you a question?"

Sam turned slowly, cautious of the strange voice and when she saw the owner of the voice, her heart did one of those stupid schoolgirl fluttery things. He was tall; his strong shoulders looked broader, encased the way they were in a well-cut suit. He ran a hand through his sandy blond hair that immediately flopped down over his forehead again. His hair was a juxtaposition to the clean-cut look he was trying to portray, but it was intriguing, and very sexy.

"Yes?" Sam drew out the word. She was pretty sure he could ask her anything and she'd be happy to answer it.

"I'm looking for a barber shop," he said. "I'm new to town."

Ah. Of course. The suit. Locals didn't walk around dressed like that. He was likely with the hotel.

She stiffened, quashing any attraction she felt for the man. "You're with the hotel." It wasn't a question.

"I am." He held out his hand. "My name is—"

"I don't care."

"Pardon?"

"Sorry," Embarrassed by her rudeness, her face reddened. "I'm just not really excited about the resort. It's not necessary."

"I don't understand. I think the resort would be bringing a lot of jobs to the town." He crossed his arms, and tilted his head, obviously amused by her. "Not to mention the tourism."

"We don't need it."

"Is that right?"

Anger and annoyance boiled through her. And something else. Something she didn't want to identify. "That's right. Now if you'll excuse me, I have work to do."

"Okay." He spoke slowly. His eyes filled with puzzlement. "But, the barber shop…"

Sam stopped herself before turning around. "It's across the street, next to the cafe. But if you ask me…"

"Yes?"

"It's fine the way it is."

She spun quickly and bit her bottom lip. What on earth made her say that? Oh, she knew exactly what made her say that. The man's eyes, his cocky smile, and his sexy shaggy hair had made her stomach flip. But it didn't matter—the man represented the enemy. She probably should have recommended Betsy at Hair Affair; she would have dyed it blue and permed it. And maybe that would be a good thing. Especially if it stopped the insane urge Sam had to run her hands through his hair.

She'd walked for five minutes, so lost in thought and chastising herself for even entertaining thoughts about a man who was in any way connected with the Springs that she didn't even realize she'd gone in the opposite direction of the Grizzly Paw. She circled back and shook her head clear of the thoughts and it wasn't until she finally set foot in her bar, after going the long way around, that she realized as annoying as the man was, he'd succeeded in distracting her from her financial troubles. At least for a few minutes.

She greeted the regulars sitting in their usual booth as she walked through her pub and back to her office where she dropped the files and sank into her chair. It had been three years since Sam Burke had given herself a migraine just by staring at the financial records for the Grizzly Paw. The difference between then and now was that three years ago, she'd just taken over operations from her father, who'd let the popular local pub fall into ruin because he was too busy drinking away his profits and chasing after any woman who'd spare his drunken ass a glance.

Three years ago, the Grizzly Paw had been in a very different situation. One that despite the roadblocks in front of her, Sam could see a way out of. She released a sigh and pulled the papers toward her again, determined to find somewhere, anywhere, she could cut back. Or even cut out. She'd already had Archer slash their food costs and despite the fact that she wouldn't know gourmet burger from a fast-food offering, she did know she liked to have a little beef between the bun. And Archer had already warned her that if she cut his budget any further, he couldn't be held responsible for what he fed the guests. Knowing him, it would probably be something he pulled out of the forest.

As if her thoughts had conjured him, there was a knock on the door and Archer blew into the room, the scent of something delicious wafting in with him.

"Sammie." He folded his large frame into the chair in front of her desk. "We need to talk."

She pushed the papers aside and tugged her long dark hair back into a ponytail in an effort to tame her unruly locks. "What can I do for you? And by the way, what's the special today? It smells delicious."

"Stew." He crossed one long leg over the other and sat back.

"Beef stew?" Her stomach rumbled with the promise of a warm meal.

"Let's just say it's stew." He raised his eyebrow and all Sam could do was shake her head and look away.

"I don't think I want to know."

"I don't think you do."

They stared at each other in a challenge for a few moments before Sam looked away. Archer was the best chef in Cedar Springs. Not only that, he was her self-proclaimed big brother and would go to the ends of the earth for her. Which is what it might come to if things didn't pick up. And when the Springs did open, with their fancy new restaurant, it was Archer's amazing food that would save them. They just needed to ride it out.

"Hello." Archer waved a hand in front of her face. "Earth to Sammie. Are you in there?"

She shook her head and narrowed her eyes. "Of course I'm in here. I was just thinking about something for a minute."

"You're going to get yourself in trouble, filling that pretty little head with thoughts." Sam sharpened her tongue, ready to spit back a sharp retort, but the smile on her friend's face gave him away. She tossed a pencil at him instead.

"Assault with a deadly weapon." He caught it deftly and tucked it behind his ear. "Well, a weapon anyway. But I'm serious—you shouldn't worry so much. You're going to get those lines on your face."

"Worry lines? They're given that name for a reason."

"Whatever. They're not hot."

Sam laughed. She had to. There was no one quite like Archer. With his big burly appearance, and his penchant for hanging out in the forest to shoot things, most people assumed he was a tough guy. But that couldn't be further from the truth. The shell might be hard, but on the inside, Archer was one of the sweetest, most sensitive men she knew. She also knew from firsthand experience, he was also fiercely protective of those he cared about. And once Archer declared him her unofficial big brother when her own brother died along with their mother when they were teenagers, and her father had become more or less useless, she'd had a protector for life. Which had proved to come in handy once or twice.

"One day you're going to make some girl very lucky," she said. "Imagine, a man who's worried about wrinkles. So selfless."

Archer held up a hand in protest. "Wait a minute. I never said anything about selfless. If you get all wrinkly, I'm going to have to look at that all day." He shuddered and Sam wished he was closer so she could smack him.

"What's up, Arch?" As much as she was enjoying the break from her stress, she still had to figure out a way to cut costs. Again. And that wasn't going to happen if she was sitting here chatting.

"I need more money."

Sam resisted the urge to hit her head against the table.

"There is no—"

"There must be. You're the only pub in town. This place is packed every night."

"If what you mean by 'packed' is a handful of tables, yes. We're packed every night."

"That's packed for Cedar Springs."

"It's not enough."

Archer tilted his head and gave Sam a look that told her he knew there was more to her stress than she was letting on. As awesome as it was to have someone who knew her so well, it was also a royal pain in the ass at times.

"Sammie." He used her nickname. "What's going on?

We've pinched pennies before, but our regulars have always been enough to keep the doors open."

She tapped her pen on the notebook in front of her. "Shouldn't you go stir that stew or something?"

He tilted his head and waited.

Sam stared at the ceiling. There wasn't any point fighting him. Archer was a lot of things, and stubborn definitely topped that list. "We need a new roof." She sat straight and stared at him. "And the furnace probably isn't going to make it through another winter. Don't even get me started on the air conditioner. We better hope for a mild summer, or the few customers we have are going to be eating outside."

"They'd like that," Archer mused. "It could be a selling feature. We have the best views in town."

"Not funny."

He reached for her hand. "It'll be fine." His voice turning serious. "It always is. You've done wonders with this place and this will work out, too. You'll see. What's the most crucial thing?"

"The roof."

"Then get it done. I'll call in some favors with my buddy Bruce. He'll give you a good deal. You have enough money for that, right?"

She did. But that's all she had, which would be fine if it wasn't for the Solstice festival that was less than a month away. Although it was the town that put on the festival, traditionally the Grizzly Paw was the headline sponsor, providing all the food, the entertainment, and of course, the venue. If she got the much-needed roof, there'd be nothing left to put on the party that the people of Cedar Springs deserved.

Sam nodded. "You're right," she said after a moment. "If Bruce can give me a deal, that would really help." There was no point telling him about the festival—he'd only worry, and both of them stressing about something there was absolutely no help for didn't seem like a good use of energy.

"So it's settled then?"

Sam looked up into Archer's smiling face. That was the thing about her long-time friend, and one of the many reasons she loved having him around. He balanced her. Sam managed a smile. "It's settled." She nodded. Logically, she knew she needed the roof. It was the right choice. She'd just have to figure everything else out later.

Chapter Two

TRENT ALWAYS HAD time to spare a nod or a friendly smile hello for his employees, and as he walked down the main corridor of the Springs, he made sure he didn't let his distracted state effect how he treated his staff. Trent prided himself on his attention to detail and as he walked through the great hall with the glass floor-to-ceiling windows, he made sure to check the water features. Some of them still weren't working properly and that was a problem. He made a mental note to discuss it with Dylan.

A water wall in the center of the hall created a tranquil barricade for a seating area with two sleek sofas. Trent knew for a fact they were extremely comfortable, while still keeping with the sleek and clean theme. The entire resort was decorated in natural colors accented with an array of blues in every shade. The overall effect was stunning and calming. Trent let his hand trail through the water of the water wall as he walked by and took his eyes off where he was going for only seconds, but it was long enough for a small boulder to slam into him and almost knock him off his feet.

"What the—"

Trent caught himself before he fell and seconds before he cursed in front of the boulder that ran into him, or more accurately, the small child who was sitting on his bottom in front of him, looking as stunned as Trent felt.

"Oh." Trent squatted down so he was at eye level with the boy. "Are you okay, little boy?"

The child whipped his head around so Trent was staring at indignant blazing eyes. "I am not a boy." The child reached up and ripped the hat from her head, exposing long blond hair.

Trent tried not to smile at the face looking up at him; her lip quivered, but there was steel in those blue eyes. "I'm so sorry," Trent said. "Clearly you are not a boy. In fact, you are a very pretty girl." The girl's eyes softened and for a second, Trent thought she might even smile at him. Instead, she pressed her lips into a tight line. He offered her a hand but she ignored him and got to her feet.

"I got it," she said. Once she was standing, it was very easy to see that she was indeed a girl, albeit one in a slightly grubby t-shirt and a ripped pair of jeans. She was about ten or eleven, not that he was very good at children's ages, and by the look of her, it had either been awhile since her last shower or she'd just been running wild in the forest. Either way, she was not the type of child Trent expected to see in the middle of the peaceful and very clean Springs resort. Especially considering they weren't even open.

"Are you lost?" he asked.

"Nope." She shook her head and looked around for an escape route. Clearly the girl, whoever she was, knew she shouldn't be there, and if Trent was a betting man, he would have put money on the fact that the child knew exactly who he was, as well. "I gotta go."

She spun on her sneakered heel to leave but Trent grabbed her arm.

"Why don't you tell me who you are before you go?"

She shook her head again and narrowed her eyes, but then her shoulders sagged in defeat. "I'm sorry. I know I'm not supposed to be in here, but I had to go to the bathroom and don't tell because my mom will kill me if she finds out. And you can't get her in trouble because it's not her fault I had to pee. She told me to go before we left and that I couldn't come in but I had to come today because school's out and she won't leave me at home 'cause of the stove thing that happened last time which wasn't my fault really but she won't believe me no matter how many times I tell her that I didn't know the spatula would melt. I mean, the other one didn't but mom says it's 'cause the other one is metal and that one was plastic. But if that's the case then it's not my fault that they're different. I mean, I can't know that stuff. I was just making a sandwich. How was I supposed to know the smoke detector would go off and the fire trucks would come? And if it wasn't mom's friend Danny who came, he's a firefighter, I would have been in even more trouble than I was if he—"

"Whoa." Trent held up a hand to ward off the never-ending monologue he never would have expected the little girl to be capable of. "That's an awfully big story." He tried to swallow a chuckle. "Especially since I don't even know your name."

She stepped forward and extended her hand. "Jules." Trent looked at her hand covered in mud, before he shook it.

"It's nice to meet you, Jules. I'm Trent Harrison and I—"

"Oh, I know who you are. You're the boss and I'm not supposed to let you see me." She tucked her hand in her pocket. "I'm real sorry. Don't tell my mom and it's not her fault. I mean it, it isn't. Normally I'd be at my grandma's house, but she had an appointment or something in the city and—"

"Okay, okay." Trent lost his battle to restrain his laughter. Whoever the kid did belong to, he was going to have to thank her for giving him a little comedic relief in the middle of such a stressful day. "If I promise not to get angry with your mom, will you tell me who she is?"

Jules eyed him suspiciously from under her dirty bangs. He held up three fingers. "Scouts' honor, she won't be in trouble."

"You were a scout?"

Trent dropped his fingers. "Well, no. Not really. But I don't lie."

"Not ever?"

"Never."

She assessed him for a moment, before finally nodding, evidently confident that he meant what he said. "Her name is Beth Martin. She's the—"

"Physical therapist."

"Yeah. And she's going to be really good at her job when you open, so—"

"I told you. She won't be in trouble." Trent held his hand out in front of him. "Why don't you come with me, and we'll go find her or at least find you something to do. Because I really don't think it's a good idea for you to be running through the hall."

Jules hung her head and trudged in the direction of the offices.

"Hey," he said. "You're not in trouble either, so don't look so worried."

"I'm not?" She glanced at him as they walked.

"No," he said. "Not this time. But if you can't be left at home, and if school's out for the summer, I think your mom may need to figure out something else when she has to work." Jules nodded solemnly. "Unless…nah."

"What?"

"Unless maybe you'd like a job at the Springs?"

"Me? I'm just a kid. What can I do?"

"Oh, I'm sure we could find something for you to do."

Trent racked his brain for something an eleven-year-old girl could do at a resort hotel. He'd have to ask Carmen for something, but despite her approach, Jules seemed like a sharp kid and more than that, she made him laugh. And that had to count for something.

"Jules!"

They both turned to see Beth, whom Trent had only met a handful of times, running toward them. She was dressed in the cool blue scrubs that were the uniform for the exercise and physical therapy staff, her blond hair pulled back into a ponytail, and her face scrubbed clean of any make-up. She was a beautiful young woman, and the few times Trent had met her, he'd been impressed with her professionalism and obvious knowledge that combined with a sweet, caring demeanor would make her popular with guests.

"Beth."

"Mom."

She came to a stop in front of them and held a hand to her chest in an effort to gain control of her breathing. "Mr. Harrison...I'm so sorry." She reached for her daughter and pulled Jules to her, shooting her a glare. "She's not supposed to be inside." She turned to Jules. "Why are you so dirty?"

"I fell out of a tree." She shrugged and tugged away from her mom.

Beth turned her attention back to Trent. "I want you to know I'd never bring my child to..."

"Work?" he finished for her. "That does appear to be what's happened here." He tried to look serious. Jules shot him a look, no doubt thinking that he'd lied to her. "I can't have children, especially muddy children, running through the halls of the Springs."

"Hey, I—"

"I am sorry, Mr. Harrison." Beth ignored her daughter's protests. "She likes to play in the forest, and she wasn't supposed to come inside. Especially since she's so dirty. It won't happen again."

"No," Trent said. "It won't." He turned to Jules and smiled at her defiant glare. "Because I've decided to hire Jules to help out a few days a week."

"Mr. Harrison, I—" Beth stopped, openmouthed and turned to Trent. "You're going to what?"

"Yeah? You're going to what?"

Trent maintained his serious composure. "Well, I can't have you running around the halls. And your mother can't have you burning the house down. So the only logical thing will be to have you work here. Maybe just for special projects? After all, we have more than enough to do before the opening. Just let Carmen know when you can come by."

Beth opened her mouth and closed it again before shaking her head. "Seriously?"

"Absolutely. Now if you'll excuse me, I was just about to head down into town to grab a bite to eat. Maybe you could tell me where I should go?" He raised his eyebrow at Beth, who still looked shocked.

She took a moment to regain her composure. "Of course. You should definitely go to the Grizzly Paw."

"The Grizzly Paw's the best," Jules said next to her. "But Mom never lets me go."

Beth shot her daughter a look and continued talking to Trent. "Sam runs the Paw now. Just say I sent you, and Archer —he's the cook—will make you the best burger you've ever had."

Trent smiled and his mouth watered a little at the thought of a good burger and a beer. The Springs had some of the best chefs he could find, and tasting their creations in the past few weeks had been great, but there was nothing like a good burger. Especially if it was accompanied by a cold beer.

"That sounds like a plan," he said, and meant it. "So, I'll

see you soon?" He pushed down on the brim of the hat Jules had replaced on her head.

"Absolutely, Mr. Harrison."

"Trent," he corrected her.

"I think Mr. Harrison will do," Beth said.

Trent looked up and met Beth's hard stare. He smirked.

"Of course," he agreed. "Well, I look forward to working with you, Jules."

He left them in the hall and took a side door so he could finish his walk outside. He hadn't been lying when he said he would go into town, and Carmen was right, he needed to spend more time in Cedar Springs. Besides that, he'd certainly liked what he'd seen when he'd gone in for a haircut. His mouth curled up at the thought of the little brunette with the spicy attitude. Obviously he couldn't guarantee running into her again, but if he could get a burger and a cold beer, he was ahead of the game. And it sounded like Sam would be just the guy to give it to him.

SAM LOOKED around the bar at the lunch crowd. Not bad. But she'd definitely prefer a few more tables full. Hopefully the regulars would keep coming once the fancy restaurant up at the Springs was officially open, with its overpriced nuggets of raw fish and dandelion salads all served up in a sterile, cold room. She scanned the walls and the antiques that she'd personally handpicked by scouring flea markets and garage sales all through Cedar Springs and the surrounding towns. As long as people continued to appreciate real cooking anymore with a cozy atmosphere where they could come and talk to their neighbors and friends, she'd be fine. She just needed to keep thinking that way.

Her customers were loyal and Sam could have hugged

every single one of them for coming in daily for Archer's soup and sandwich special. It was the regulars who were keeping her in business and without them...well, she didn't want to think about it.

And she wouldn't. Instead of worrying, she kept herself busy behind the bar. Sam organized and wiped down the liquor bottles for the second time that day. Cleaning helped her think—which meant that lately, she had a very clean bar. It seemed that all she ever did lately was think about things. How to make money. How to save money. How to pull money from her—

"Aren't you a sight for sore eyes."

One hand on a bottle and one hand on the rag, she froze. She knew that voice. It belonged to someone she hadn't seen in a long time. The hair on the back of Sam's neck stood up. Knowing what she'd be facing, she swallowed hard and looked up anyway. He stood on the other side of the bar; only a slab of polished mahogany stood between them. It should have been enough, but when she looked into his crystal blue eyes that had a way of seeing right through her into the very heart of her being, it wasn't enough. Not nearly enough. All the old feelings tried to come back. But she wasn't going to let them. Not this time.

"Preston." Caught off guard, her voice sounded small and she hated herself for it. Sam swallowed hard and tried again. "What are you doing here?" She forced a hardness into her voice.

No answer would be adequate. No explanation why the boy she'd given herself to, thought she would be with forever and swore her love to, only to have him walk out and leave her lonely and heartbroken was back in town would be good enough.

He leaned against the bar. "What if I told you I came here to see you?"

She straightened her shoulders and regained her senses. "Then I'd know you were lying. I suppose your mom made you come." She squeezed the cloth in her hands and furiously scrubbed at a spot on the wood.

"I wanted to come. I missed you."

Sam knew he was lying. It was always the same with Preston. Ever since they were teenagers, he knew what to say to make her melt and she did. Every time. It was infuriating. No matter what she tried and what her brain tried to tell her, her body reacted in a completely different way. When he spoke, she responded. She always had.

But not this time. Time had hardened her, made her see clearly.

"I'm sure you've been far too busy in the city to miss me at all." She stopped scrubbing at the spot that didn't seem to want to come clean anyway, and shifted her attention to the glasses in the washer. She gave each one a quick polish as she pulled them out and placed them on the shelf. "In fact," she said, as if she needed to torture herself with his response, "I'm sure you've barely given me a thought since the last time you left." Sadly, it hadn't been the first time Preston Mackelroy had come into the Grizzly Paw wanting to pick up where they'd left off, even if it was for a night or two. Sam wasn't proud of it; she'd made her share of bad choices when it came to Preston. The first time, he'd left her when it mattered the most. After her mom and brother had died, she'd needed him, but he wasn't going to let anything stop his dreams of moving to the city. Especially not his broken-hearted girlfriend. The only one she could blame for the other times was herself. But she was done.

"Sam, I'm never too busy for you." He reached across the bar and took a strand of her dark hair in his fingers, letting it slide through his grasp. She fought hard to control the shivers that blasted through her. He would not get to her. Not this time. She was too smart for him. "In fact," he continued, "I

24

was hoping we could catch up while I'm here." His hand slid alongside her cheek but instead of sinking into the sensation, she pulled away. "Come on, I'm only here for a few nights, and I know we have a lot of catching up to do, don't we?"

She shook her head. No. It had taken her months to recover from his last visit and she'd sworn to herself that she'd never do it again. She was too strong of a woman to fall for that over and over again.

"I thought I told you that you weren't welcome in here again, Mackelroy."

Sam turned to see Archer standing in the doorway to the kitchen, his arms crossed tightly over his chest, a glare in his eyes. There had never been any love lost between the two men, but after the last time Preston had left her heart fractured, it was Archer who put it back together again. He'd spent hours with her convincing her she deserved better and there was someone out there for her that would treat her right.

As if he read her thoughts, Archer shot her a look. "I need to see you in the kitchen, Sam."

"Now?" She glanced between the men.

"Now. It's an emergency."

"An emergency?"

"You need someone to stir your soup, Wolfe?"

Archer took a step toward Preston and for a second Sam was afraid he might hit him, but Archer stopped himself, and turned to her. "Now," he said through gritted teeth.

She sighed. There really wasn't any point pushing Archer further. "Fine. I'll be right back," she said to Preston. "Don't get into any trouble while I'm gone."

"Without you?" He wiggled his eyebrow in a way that used to make her stomach flip, but to her surprise, only made her shake her head. Maybe she really was starting to get over him?

Sam followed Archer through the swinging kitchen door and before it even had time to swing shut behind her, he spun around to confront her. "What do you think you're doing? You shouldn't even let that asshole through the door after the way he treated you."

"It's not like that, Arch." She rolled her shoulders and stared up at the ceiling. "I'm just being friendly."

"He made his choice a long time ago." Archer continued as if she hadn't spoken at all. "You weren't good enough for him then, what makes you think you're good enough now?"

His words cut deep. "Thanks."

"You know what I mean."

"Oh I know." Sam picked up a stack of napkins and rolled some cutlery. "I'm just some piece of townie trash. Not good enough for much more than slinging drinks and serving up greasy burgers."

"No." Archer grabbed her by both shoulders and shook her gently. "That's not true, and you damn well know it. Preston has never been good enough for you. Not the other way around. You deserve a hell of a lot better than that self-centered piece of—"

"I got it, Arch." She shrugged him off and rolled another set of cutlery. "You beat that into my head years ago. He doesn't deserve me, I can do better, yeah, yeah."

"It's true, Sam."

"You know what I believe?" She tossed a fork back into the cutlery pile. "I believe that I'm sick of living like a nun. Some-times a girl just wants to—"

"Spare me the details, please." He put his hands over his ears and hummed, making her laugh until she swatted him with a towel.

"Okay, okay. I get it."

"Promise me you'll stay away from Preston."

It wasn't a hard promise to keep. "Okay," she agreed. "I'll stay away from him."

Archer smiled. "Good." He wiped his hands on his apron in anticipation. "I'll go get rid of him."

"I don't need you to do that."

Her friend raised an eyebrow because they both knew that was a lie.

"Oh, and for the record, I don't make greasy burgers." Archer untied his apron and threw it at her. "Don't look so bummed, Sam. I'm sure some guy is going to come along and give you all kinds of pleasures I'm never going to want to hear about."

Chapter Three

FROM THE OUTSIDE, the Grizzly Paw was everything Trent expected it to be. A typical small-town pub in a mountain town, it had wooden siding, with a generous front porch and big windows on either side of the door. The cedar shingles were grayed and in some spots the roof looked like it had been completely taken over by the surrounding pine trees, it blended in so well. It was rustic, and despite the fact that he tended to prefer a more modern and sleek style, Trent liked it. And you couldn't beat the location. A large grassy field spilled out to the lake beyond, giving the place perfect views. He walked up the steps, trailed his hands over bright blossoms of some red flower he couldn't identify that filled some large pots, and opened the door.

The second he stepped inside, the aroma of home cooking immediately hit him instead of the expected smell of stale smoke and spilled beer. His stomach rumbled and he remembered what Beth had said about the Grizzly Paw making a great burger.

As he walked through the room, he glanced around at the tables that were occupied. People seemed to be enjoying their lunches and were chatting comfortably. He smiled and nodded as he made his way to the bar, choosing the more social option instead of the tables with the excellent views by the window. Carmen was right; he needed to get out more. He pulled up a stool and sat down next to the only other man sitting at the bar.

"Hey." Trent tried to keep his tone light and friendly. "Is there a bartender around here?"

"Yeah." The man nodded and focused his attention on the door behind the bar. "Sam's just in the back there."

"Great." He didn't seem like he was up for chatting, but Trent thought he'd give it one more try. "Do you live in—"

Before he could finish what he was going to say, the door to the kitchen swung open and a large man pushed through. "Time to go, Preston." He stood with his arms crossed and stared at the man next to Trent, who opened his mouth, but, obviously decided to keep his thoughts to himself and closed it again before he stood.

Trent watched the mostly silent exchange with interest. A little local drama was always entertaining, and as long as it didn't involve him, he was all for it.

"You're not welcome in here, Preston," the man behind the bar, whom Trent could only assume was Sam, said. "I don't want to see your face again."

"I'll go," the other man said. "But we both know that decision isn't yours to make. She's a big girl."

"Get out."

Trent stood and squared himself for a fight, instinctually ready to back up the bartender. The man flicked his gaze between Trent and his adversary and decided he wasn't up for a fight.

"Best for you to leave town altogether."

"I don't know," Preston said. "I might just stick around

until the festival. Things always get more interesting around the solstice. And we all know about the kiss—"

A growl escaped the man behind the bar and for a moment, Trent thought he might come right over and make the other man leave.

"Time to go." Trent nodded his head. He expected more of a fight, but to his surprise, Preston grinned and walked out.

When he was gone, the air seemed to clear and Trent returned to his seat, more than ready for that beer.

"Thanks for backing me up there. What can I get you to drink?"

"Hey," Trent said. "It was no problem. Besides, I don't think you needed any help from me. But if it's all the same, I'd love a beer."

"Coming right up."

Trent watched while the man poured a beer and set the frothy mug in front of him.

"You must be Sam." He lifted the glass to his lips, enjoying the icy goodness. It'd been a long time since he'd had a cold one, and it was exactly what he needed. The man raised his eyebrows, and took a step back, crossing his arms over his chest, but didn't say anything, so Trent continued, "I heard the Grizzly Paw had the best burgers in town."

"Well, that's a true story," the man said. "Best burgers for miles. And you won't get food like this up the hill."

Trent stiffened, but forced himself to relax. It wouldn't do any good to get defensive. He was there to make friends. "Funny you mention the Springs." He said the next words as casually as he could manage. "I'm one of the owners up there."

"You don't say?" The man smirked and Trent met his gaze, neither of them willing to lose any ground as a silent and unexpected battle of wills warred between them.

He'd expected some sort of resistance, and he was

prepared to hold his own. Careful to stay as non-confrontational as possible, Trent waited while the other man formed his opinion of him. After a moment, he smiled, and stuck out his hand. "I'm Archer. I can help you with that burger and I'll go get Sam for you."

Trent matched his smile and took another gulp of his beer. "I appreciate it."

Archer disappeared into the kitchen and Trent took the opportunity to finish his beer and look around the room. An elderly man in a corner booth was just finishing up his meal and looked like he was getting ready to leave. Trent glanced around. There wasn't a waitress in sight and he kept a close watch on the man in case he decided to split on his bill. He'd seen enough of that type of thing in his years in the restaurant and hotel industry, and he definitely recognized the signs.

The old man stood, stretched and fussed around with his jacket for a few minutes. Trent was just about to go over to him when the kitchen door opened and an extremely beautiful woman appeared. A woman he'd seen before.

"What can I do for…oh," she said. "It's you." There was no malice in her voice, just a slight tinge of irritation. But her full, pink lips turned up in a smile and she brushed a stray strand of hair off her cheek and tucked it behind her ear.

His own grin was an automatic response and he wasn't even going to pretend he wasn't happy to see her again. Meeting her on the street had been brief, but there was something about the woman and the way she'd looked at him then, and was looking at him now, that intrigued him. "I would love another beer." He leaned an elbow on the bar. "But that man over there looks like he's getting ready to walk out on his bill."

"Who? Him?" Her chocolate eyes followed to where Trent gestured. "Miles," she called. "How was lunch?"

The old man turned in her direction and smiled a toothy grin. "Could use a few more pickles next time."

"I'll keep that in mind," she said. "Have a good day, Miles."

The old man nodded and shuffled out of the bar.

"He didn't pay," Trent said. "Shouldn't you be—"

"Miles has a tab." The waitress grabbed Trent's glass, filled it from the tap, put it in front of him again and wiped the counter. "He comes in every day for lunch. But I appreciate your concern."

"I've seen too many waitresses lose out." He lifted his mug and watched her over the glass. Her jeans were snug, showcasing a tight body, with a simple black t-shirt that dipped low in the front and gave him a very tempting view of the swell of her breast. He shifted in his seat. Maybe it wasn't such a bad idea after all to start getting to know the people of Cedar Springs. "It's nice to run into you again," he said.

She gave him a wary smile.

"I guess it's my good luck that you work here," Trent said. "Maybe we could—"

"Archer said you wanted to talk to—"

"Sam, yes," he cut her off. "But I'd love to get to know you better, too. I'm Trent." He held out his hand but she didn't take it.

"Sam." Her clipped tone said it all. "Samantha, actually."

"Oh." He retracted his hand, a bit dumbfounded. "I...I didn't—"

"Expect a woman?" She put one hand on her hip, which not only had the effect of making her look extremely pissed off, but also made her look extremely hot, His body came to attention.

"No," he answered honestly. "I didn't expect a woman. I just assumed that—"

"I was some dumb waitress who would let my checks walk out on me?"

Her annoyance combined with her habit of cutting him off

was starting to piss him off, and turn him on, but he wasn't going to admit that. "I was just trying to help," he said. "I thought I made that clear."

"I don't need your help."

She spun around and with her back to him, wiped down the counter and organized the glasses.

"Look, I didn't mean any offense," he tried again. "To be fair, no one told me Sam was a woman and it's not really the type of name that would lead me to believe any differently."

She stopped moving, which Trent took to be a sign that she might be listening to him and possibly giving him a chance to salvage the mess of the situation he'd created. "Beth sent me down here," he continued.

"Beth?" She still didn't turn around.

"Yes. She said the Grizzly Paw had the best burgers around and if I mentioned she sent me, you'd be nice to me." Surely it wouldn't hurt to elaborate a little bit, Trent decided. Besides, Beth owed him for going so easy on Jules.

"She said that?"

"Yes."

Slowly, Samantha, as he'd decided to refer to her because it was so much safer, turned around again. He saw judgment in her eyes, but something else, too. Interest, maybe? Possibly not, but it didn't stop a guy from trying. And there was something about the dark-eyed beauty that definitely made Trent want to try.

SOMETHING about the man sitting in front of her made Sam uneasy. Over the years she'd run into her fair share of men who unsettled her or challenged her. Usually they'd had too much to drink and got sloppy, or were incessantly hitting on her. But none of the men she'd had to deal with at the Grizzly

Paw made her nervous the way that Trent did sitting in front of her. She couldn't put her finger on it, and that was the part that made her crazy.

"Beth was right about the burgers." She tried to act as naturally as possible and forced the butterflies in her stomach away. "Archer said he was going to make you one."

He nodded and that same flop of sandy blond hair fell over his eyebrow. He didn't get his hair cut after all, and something about that thrilled her. He didn't swipe it back right away and Sam was glad because it gave his otherwise perfectly groomed look a bit of casual, and she liked it. Besides, she had an over-whelming urge to reach out and smooth it back herself so she could see the deep green of his eyes a little more clearly. Not that she would. She shook her head and tried to refocus on wiping the countertop. Anything to keep her distracted from the incredibly handsome man in front of her and the incred-ibly annoying and persistent thought of what it would be like to kiss him.

"I'm looking forward to it."

Sam's head shot up. "Pardon me?" Had she spoken out loud? Her face burned from the embarrassment, but Trent smiled and gave her a strange glance.

"The burger," he said. "I'm looking forward to it."

"Of course."

"What did you think I meant?"

Sam refused to look up again. At least not until the earth opened up and swallowed her. She was acting like a schoolgirl. A schoolgirl whose hormones were shooting out of control. It had to be because of Preston. If he hadn't shown up out of the blue, she wouldn't be reacting to this total stranger the way she was. Preston always had that effect on her, and...

The bell from the back that signaled the burger was ready sounded, and saved Sam from herself.

"I'll be right back." She hoped she sounded much more in

control of herself than she felt. It wasn't until she pushed through the kitchen door that she realized she'd never asked Trent why he'd been talking to Beth about her at all. Maybe she could get Archer to take his food out? That way she could go back to her office and depress herself further with the financials and save herself from further embarrassment.

"What's up with you?"

Sam blinked hard and looked up at Archer, who was staring at her with a bemused expression. She ignored both his comment and the way he was laughing at her. "I need you to take that to the guy at the bar." She pointed to the burger and filled a glass of water at the sink, drinking it down in an effort to quench the fire that was suddenly and intensely burning inside her.

"No can do."

Sam spun around. "What do you mean, no?"

"I mean no. Too busy."

Sam looked around the kitchen. With lunch long over, and no new customers, Archer was definitely not busy and they both knew it.

"Doing what?"

"Cleaning."

The kitchen was pristine, as it always was. Archer took a great deal of pride in his work and that included keeping his space immaculate. Sam raised an eyebrow. "Archer, I'm your boss." She put her hands on her hips and tried her best to look tough. "And I'm telling you to take the customer his lunch."

"If by customer, you mean the man at the bar who happens to own the Springs," he paused, gauging her reaction, "the answer is still no."

Her first response was to get angry and assert her dominance as the owner and the one who signed Archer's checks, but something he said caught her attention. "What do you mean, owner of the Springs?"

Sam hated the Springs and everything they represented in her hometown. The resort on the top of the hill was pretentious, and soon it would be full of rich, over-indulged people who had nothing better to do with their time than spend it soaking in some hot water that apparently had magical healing properties. And the con artists responsible for building and operating the place were not only crooks, but they'd invaded her peaceful town and were going to be single-handedly responsible for ruining her business and bringing in even more outsiders. The thought that Trent—who was not only gorgeous with his deep green eyes and broad shoulders that she'd wanted to run her hands across from the moment she'd met him, but also caused a stir deep in her belly that she hadn't felt for a very long time—could not only be associated with the Springs, but responsible for it, made her stomach turn.

"I mean, he's one of the two Harrison brothers who have brought the resort into our towns and our hearts." Archer clutched his chest in an elaborate pantomime.

Sam picked up a hand towel and chucked it at him. "Cut it out."

He caught it expertly and tucked it into his apron. "I don't know why you hate the resort so much, Sam. It's not the devil. If you stopped to think about it, I think you'd see it's a good thing for Cedar Springs."

"Name one good thing."

"Beth likes it up there."

Beth was Sam's best friend, and as much as she valued her opinion, Sam knew she was biased. For Beth, the job opening at the Springs was a lifeline for her and her daughter. It meant she could move back home from the city so she could raise Jules in her hometown. Before the Springs opened, there was no place for a physiotherapist in a small town. And as much as she loved having her best friend home again, Sam still couldn't bring herself to be okay with the resort, especially the people who'd brought it to her private piece of paradise. Especially when those people stirred up such unexpected and strong feelings inside her. No, there was no way she could ever imagine a world where she'd ever warm up to Trent Harrison or his stupid resort.

"Take him the burger," she said. "I'll be in my office."

Before Archer could protest again, Sam stormed out of the kitchen and into the tiny back room she was growing to hate. She locked the door behind her, slid into her chair and dropped her head into her hands. Her eyes fell on the stack of bills that never seemed to go anywhere and she couldn't decide whether she was angrier at Trent Harrison for his role in the resort that was causing all her problems, or herself for being drawn to him like an ant to honey.

Chapter Four

ALL TOO SOON THE doors to the Springs would be open to the public, and Trent's quiet mornings of walking the grounds would be gone. Not that he'd be too sad. He was probably more anxious than anyone else to get things rolling. And he had no doubt they'd be rolling. As soon as word got out about the natural healing properties of the hot pools, and once their well-placed advertising campaigns started, the Springs would be fully booked. He had no doubt of that.

Taking a detour to the main desk, Trent walked past the six-story glass wall that showcased the tranquil pools inside. They'd managed to harness the water and channel it into an indoor spa-styled pool where guests could soak in the healing waters. The natural water that bubbled out of the earth was a hundred and eight degrees, which could be a bit much for some guests, so they'd made sure to construct a variety of soaking pools so the water temperature could be adjusted to accommodate all guests. There was even a plunge pool where the temperature was only a few shades off freezing. At least, it felt that way to Trent. But they'd wanted to be sure to appeal to everyone.

The empty pools bubbled away, ready for the guests who would soon be able to enjoy them at all hours of the day. Trent was adamant about not putting any restrictions on using the facilities for guests. They were open twenty-four hours a day because for some, healing took place in the middle of the night. He stopped in front of the glass wall and gazed around the facility. It was stunning and the glow of pride Trent felt every time he looked at what his vision had built was unmistakable. But that glow was dimming. Les Braxton was still on him. He wasn't going to be happy until the entire hotel was booked solid, but even Trent knew that was an ambitious goal for the first few months. The man needed to be patient.

With a sigh of frustration, Trent left the pools behind and kept walking. Maybe if there was more support from the locals, they could bill the Springs as an entire experience, with artisan shopping in town and a tranquil small-town getaway. But there were still those in town who viewed him as the enemy. Carmen was right; he needed to do something nice for Cedar Springs. Show the town that they were here to stay, as partners. He'd overheard something about a festival that would be taking place for the summer solstice. That might be just the thing and maybe he could ask Samantha Burke about it. She seemed to know what was going on in town.

The heat in his gut that was becoming all too familiar every time he thought of the attractive bar owner with an edge caught his attention. In an attempt to cool his thoughts, Trent slipped out a side door and into the meditation gardens. Or what would be the meditation gardens as soon as the gardeners he'd hired finished their work. Which they were slated to do later in the week.

For the last three days since he'd ventured into town, into the Grizzly Paw and straight into the life of Samantha Burke, all he could think about was the way her lips pouted when she spoke to him, and the sharp way she held her shoulders in an effort to look in control, or the intense need he saw in her impossibly dark eyes when she looked at him. It wasn't his imagination. He recognized carefully leashed desire when he saw it. And he'd definitely seen it. Now he just needed to see it again. After finishing his burger, he'd waited for her to reappear, but she never had and eventually Trent had to return to work. Had she been avoiding him because she felt the heat between them too? The thought consumed him.

He strode absently along the cobblestone path, thoughts of Samantha occupying his mind. If he hadn't been so preoccupied by the woman, he might have noticed that the flash of movement he saw out of the corner of his eyes was more than just a bird. When the streak of yellow appeared in his peripheral vision again, Trent froze. That was no bird.

It was too early for anyone to be in the gardens, and the workers weren't scheduled to show up until eight. A quick glance at his watch told Trent he still had two more hours before they'd be there. Which left one option. An intruder.

He ducked low, and moved toward a large barrel full of decorative stone. Crouching beside it, Trent glanced around the side and scanned the garden. The early morning shadows made it difficult to see, but there was no mistaking the streak of yellow that darted out and behind a shrub. Without thinking, Trent launched himself up and with a few quick strides, reached the intruder and grabbed him by the collar.

"What do you think you're doing here, ass—"

The words died on his lips as he looked down into the frightened eyes of Jules. He released her collar but kept a tight grip on her arm. "Jules?"

"I'm sorry." The girl's eyes darted around like a wild rabbit looking for an escape route. "I didn't mean for you to see me. I was just…I'm sorry."

"What are you doing here so early? It's freezing." He realized for the first time just how cool it was in the mountains predawn. "And it's Saturday. Your mom doesn't work today, does she?"

Truthfully, Trent had no idea when Beth worked. But he did know that Jules wasn't scheduled to work with Carmen until Monday.

"No, she doesn't." Jules still would not meet his gaze. "And she doesn't know I'm here. But I…I…look," she met his eyes for the first time and Trent could see the defiance, clouding an underlying sadness reflected back at him, "I know I'm not supposed to be here, okay. But my mom wants me to go meet other kids and…I like it here better. It's relaxing and…peaceful."

Trent released her, confident she wouldn't be running after her confession. "It is peaceful, I agree. But it wouldn't be that way if I just let random children run around, would it?"

She put her hands on her hips and stuck her chest out. "I'm not random."

"Not to me." Trent raised his eyebrow. "But to pretty much anyone else around here, you're random. And I can't have you out here. It's not safe." He blew his breath into his hands and rubbed his shirtsleeves. "Besides that, it's freezing. Come on. I'll get you some breakfast."

Jules looked at him suspiciously, as if he had some sort of hidden agenda. The truth was, he didn't. Something about the spunky little girl amused him, and he admired her determination. It would serve her well in life.

"Really," he said when she still hadn't moved. "I haven't eaten yet, either. And the chefs are busy prepping. They're always happy to actually cook something. Let's go."

Together they walked through the halls, and as there were only a few workers milling about, they didn't attract any attention. Trent's eye landed on a low fountain that wasn't running. He stopped and made a note. That was the third water feature he'd noticed that wasn't working properly. He'd have to talk to Kurt, his head maintenance guy.

A few minutes later, they were seated at a corner table in Stillwater, the resort's cafe, and he'd placed their order for two stacks of pancakes with a coffee for him and an orange juice for her. Jax, the head chef, was more than happy to whip up some breakfast. After he got their drinks and placed it in front of Jules, Trent asked, "Does your mother know you're here?"

The way Jules looked down at the table and picked at her napkin was all the answer he needed.

"You'll need to call her," he said. "She'll be worried."

"No she won't. She's too busy with her new career to care about me. She thinks I'll just make friends and everything will be fine. But the kids here are different than in the city. They won't like me."

And in that moment, Trent saw what the real problem with his new delinquent friend was. "Change can be pretty hard, huh?"

Jules nodded but didn't look up.

"What did she do before she came to work here?" He tried to remember what Beth's personnel file said, but truthfully, he didn't spend much time with the dealings of the staff. That was Carmen's department.

"We lived in the city," Jules said. "We lived in a tiny apartment and she worked at the hospital."

"And your dad?"

Her face shot up, her eyes blazing. "I don't have a dad."

Trent nodded and took a sip of his coffee. "Gotcha." He waited a beat before prying a bit more. "So why did you move here?"

"Mom grew up here and when this was built," she waved her skinny arm around, "she got the job and we came here. She keeps saying how much I'm going to like it here and what a great childhood she had. But I don't get it. Cedar Springs sucks."

Trent tried not to smile.

"Except for Auntie Sam. She's okay."

Trent froze. Auntie Sam? "You mean Samantha who owns the Grizzly Paw?" He hoped he sounded a lot more casual than he felt. "Where you told me to go for a burger?"

"Yeah." At that moment, Jax came and put two towering stacks of pancakes in front of them, along with a side plate of fresh butter and syrup. "Did you have the burger there? I told you it was the best, right?"

Jax glanced at Trent, as if he, too, was waiting for the answer.

He nodded. "I did," he answered Jules. "You were right. It's the best burger I've ever had." Looking to the chef, he added, "With the exception of yours, of course."

"Whatever you say," the chef said good-naturedly. "It's a good thing hamburgers aren't my specialty or I'd take offense." He laughed. "Enjoy your breakfast."

"And it was good, right?" Jules asked, her mouth full of pancakes.

"It was. But tell me about your auntie." Trent knew it had to be a bad idea to ask a kid about a woman, but there didn't seem to be a lot of options open to him, and she was here and... "Is she your mom's sister?"

"Nah. She's not really my auntie but she's Mom's best friend, so close enough."

Trent nodded. "And is there an uncle?" He tried to sound casual, but he knew he'd failed in his attempt when Jules put down her fork and gave him a strange look over the top of her glass of juice.

"You mean, like, is Auntie Sam married?"

He shrugged and focused on cutting his pancakes.

"She's not," Jules said, and a thrill that was more annoying

43

than anything else flashed through him. "But Mom said her boyfriend's back in town." And just like that, the thrill was gone.

"Boyfriend?"

Jules shrugged and shoved more pancake in her mouth. "Never met him. But hey," she said, changing tack. "Maybe he'll be at the festival? Auntie Sam does it every year. I only got to go once when I was a kid, but now that we live here…should be fun, I guess."

"That sounds interesting," he mused. "I heard something about it the other day." The kernel of an idea that'd started to form earlier took shape. "Tell me what you remember about the festival," he said. "And what do you mean, Samantha does it every year?"

"I DON'T KNOW what you're thinking." Beth's voice called out from the bedroom. Sam didn't even bother asking her best friend what she was referring to because she knew exactly what her friend was talking about. Instead, she flopped down on Beth's couch and picked up a magazine. She pretended to look at the pages while her friend continued to talk from the other room. "He wasn't any good for you when we were in high school, and he's really no good for you now."

Beth appeared in the doorway, wearing a blue sundress that complemented her eyes perfectly. "You look fantastic," Sam said, and meant it. "Where did you get that? Because I know for a fact that Cedar Springs certainly doesn't have any stores that sell clothes like that."

"I ordered it." Her friend twirled, showing off her legs. "I probably shouldn't have spent so much, but I couldn't help it. I thought it would be perfect for the festival. I'll be more than ready to dance the night away. And you never know…maybe

I'll actually find someone to kiss after the toast. I can't believe it's been so long since I've been able to go, and from everything I heard, you know how to do it right."

At the mention of the festival, Sam shrank back into the couch. She knew Beth and half the town had been looking forward to a big party to kick off the summer season. The year before, she'd managed to convince a half decent band to come from the city and even though it'd cost way more than she should have spent, it was worth it, especially considering it had been the first festival she'd thrown on her own since taking over the Grizzly Paw. The problem was, now everyone in Cedar Springs expected the same level of entertainment.

"The dress is perfect." Sam tossed the magazine on the table and sat up. "But why are you worrying about kissing someone? Besides, it's just a stupid legend."

The legend was that whomever you kissed at the solstice festival, immediately after the toast when the paper lanterns were released, would be your sweetheart for the season. Sam had never kissed anyone, which may have been the problem.

"It is not," Beth protested. "Now, don't avoid the question."

"I didn't hear a question."

Beth poured them each a glass of lemonade and handed one to Sam. "Don't be stupid." She sat across from her. "We're talking about Preston."

"Are we?"

Beth ignored her. "I heard he's in town," she said. "And I also heard he's been to the Paw to visit you, so don't even pretend you don't know what I'm talking about."

"I'm going to kill Archer." When it came to her love life, he seemed to think he needed to play the role of protector, and in Archer's world, that included giving all the details to Beth so they could team up on her.

"Don't blame Archer." Beth took a sip of her drink and stared at Sam. "But he's right. Preston's a jerk and you better not have any ideas of hooking up with him just because he's back for a little bit."

The truth was, Sam might have entertained the idea of Preston for a minute or two, mostly because he was familiar and comfortable. But for the last few nights, when she laid in her bed alone, it wasn't Preston's face she saw when she closed her eyes.

"Quite honestly, I'm totally over it. He just doesn't know it yet. Speaking of being back in Cedar Springs." Sam needed to change the subject. "How's it going? How's Jules doing?" She looked out the window at the girl lounging in a deck chair and staring at her tablet.

Beth sighed and dropped her head in her hands. "Jules hates it. I keep wondering if I did the right thing coming back and taking her away from all her friends. But it was so hard in the city with just the two of us. It has to be better with family and good friends around, right?"

Sam nodded, although she had absolutely no idea whether Beth was right or not. She'd always admired her best friend for raising Jules on her own. It hadn't been easy for her as a teenager with a baby, alone. But she'd managed to finish school and take her training to become a physiotherapist and through everything, Beth had always put her daughter first. "She's a good kid," Sam said. "She'll be okay as soon as school starts and she starts to make friends."

"She could make friends now if she didn't insist on running up to the Springs every chance she got. She hates staying with her grandma, and I can't leave her alone after—"

"I remember." Sam couldn't help the laugh that escaped her as she thought of the time Jules almost lit the house on fire. Beth glared at her and Sam swallowed her laughter. "What do you mean, she's running up to the Springs? What's she doing up there?"

"She's made a friend." Beth raised her eyebrows and

pushed out of the chair, and headed back to the bedroom. "Hold on, I have to change."

"A friend? At a snooty resort?"

"It's not snooty," she called.

"Whatever," Sam mumbled under her breath and reached for a bowl of nuts on the table. "So who's the friend?" She popped an almond in her mouth.

"Trent Harrison."

The almond caught in her throat and she coughed hard to dislodge it. "Trent?" She choked out the word when she got control of herself.

"You okay?" Beth poked her head out of the bedroom.

"Fine. What do you mean Jules is friends with Trent Harrison? Isn't he the owner or something?"

Beth pulled a t-shirt over her head and joined Sam on the couch. She took the bowl of nuts from her. "Yup. Have you met him?"

She nodded and immediately cursed her body for the heated flush that crept over her skin at the mere thought of Trent Harrison. She could only hope Beth hadn't noticed her reaction or she'd never hear the end of it. "He came into the Grizzly Paw and—"

"Ordered a burger?"

"How did you know?" She raised an eyebrow in suspicion at her friend and grabbed a handful of nuts.

"I told him you had the best burgers in town. Besides, he's pretty cute, don't you think?"

"I hadn't noticed." She stuffed the nuts in her mouth and wouldn't look at Beth.

"Oh yes you did."

Sam shook her head.

"He's gorgeous, Sam. And you should see the way he is with Jules, he's so…"

"Don't tell me you're falling for your boss." The idea horrified her. But not because Beth shouldn't be hitting on her boss, which she shouldn't, but because if Beth did have a crush on him, she'd never be able to admit that she couldn't stop thinking about the man since the moment he'd set foot in her bar. And those feelings were far from platonic. Despite the fact that he represented everything she hated.

"No." Beth laughed and swatted her arm. "He's not my type at all. And there's no way I'm going to screw up the only physio job in town. Whether Jules likes it or not, we're here to stay."

Relief flooded through her, and Sam dropped her head onto Beth's shoulder. "Good. I missed you."

"Besides," Beth said. "I'd never go after a man you're so clearly into."

Sam shot up and off the couch, staring at her friend, open-mouthed. "I don't know what…you're crazy, I…why would you…ugh."

"I've known you a long time, Samantha Burke, and I'm not blind. And quite honestly, I think it's great. You haven't dated anyone since Preston, and you're way too young and hot to live like a nun."

"I could say the same."

"You aren't a mother. You have no excuse."

"I'm a busy business owner." Sam grabbed her purse, before Beth started digging into feelings she couldn't even explain. "Speaking of which. I should go. I can't leave Archer in charge for too long or he'll revolt."

She waved to Jules as she made her way to her truck.

The girl put her tablet down and jogged toward Sam. "Wait up for a second. Did you meet my friend Trent yet?"

Sam's face flushed again, and she nodded. "I did. But I didn't know he was your friend. What are you doing hanging out with adults? Shouldn't you be looking for friends your own age?"

"Whatever. He's cool, though, right? And he gave me a job. I'm going to be working at the Springs a few days a week."

"Aren't you a little young for a job?" Sam tried to keep her voice light, especially when the kid she thought of as her niece was clearly excited about it. "Shouldn't you be hanging out and having fun this summer? There's plenty of time to work when you're older. And you could always help out at the Paw if you really want something to do."

Jules shrugged. "Nah. I like the Springs." Sam tried to keep the hurt off her face. There was no way Jules could know that she hated the resort she so clearly loved, or the man she now idolized. Not that it was hate exactly that she felt for Trent, but...

"Whatever you say, kiddo. I gotta run, but promise you'll come hang out with me soon, okay?"

"Totally. Maybe Trent can come, too. He said he loved the burger."

"Did he?" Sam muttered more to herself since Jules had already turned and jogged back to her chair and her waiting tablet. "Did he really?"

SHE WAS STILL THINKING about Trent and the annoying way he managed to nose his way into every aspect of her life when she walked into the bar. Preoccupied by her thoughts, she didn't notice Preston hunkered down in a corner booth until he practically jumped out at her.

"What the hell, Preston." Sam put her hands up as a reflex to ward him off. "What are you doing?"

"I didn't mean to scare you, Sammie." Preston deftly slipped his arms around her and pulled her into his chest. He smelled good. Familiar. And it annoyed her that she thought so. "I was waiting for you to get back."

She ducked down and slipped under his arms. "Why are you waiting back here? Sit up at the bar like a normal person."

Preston flicked his gaze toward the bar and Archer, who'd noticed the commotion and didn't look very happy.

"Ah," she said. "Archer said something to you, didn't he?" She shook her head. No matter how she may feel or not feel about Preston, she was going to have to have words with Archer about his involvement in her personal life. It was ridiculous. "Come on."

For a minute, she didn't think he was going to follow, which definitely said something about how badly Archer had threatened him, or Preston's lack of courage. Or both. Either way, she was not impressed.

Archer opened his mouth to object to Preston's presence, but Sam cut him off before he could say anything. "Everyone's welcome in my bar, Archer." She glanced between the two men, her eyes resting on Archer. "Everyone."

"Whatever you say, boss."

Preston settled onto a bar stool, and when Archer didn't make any move to serve him, Sam asked, "What can I get you?"

"I actually came to talk to you, Sam. I miss you."

Sam didn't miss the way Archer's back stiffened, and she was pretty sure if she listened carefully, she'd be able to hear him growl, too.

"Look." She ignored Archer and addressed Preston. "I'm really busy right now and—"

"With the festival, I know. And like I said…" He reached across the bar and stroked the skin over her thumb the way he used to. To her surprise, instead of enjoying his touch the way she normally did, it grated on her. "I want to help however I can," he finished.

She pulled her hand away. "I appreciate it, but—"

"Oh." Archer interrupted them. "I almost forgot. Trent Harrison called for you."

"Trent?"

"Who?"

"He said something about the festival and a band."

Sam's mind spun to keep up with what Archer was saying. In the few minutes she'd spoken to Trent, she'd certainly not mentioned the festival to him, and she had definitely not mentioned a band, because this year, the only musical entertainment she was going to be able to afford was the jukebox next to the pool table. And even then festival-goers would have to supply the quarters. What game was he trying to play? As if it wasn't bad enough that he moved his big resort into town, now he was trying to nose in on her festival.

"Here." Archer thrust a piece of paper toward her. "He left his number and said to call as soon as you got in."

The numbers on the paper blurred as Sam thought of the man who'd be on the other end of the line when she dialed them. His deep voice and the way her name sounded when he said it. Smooth and sensual and... "I should go see him," she announced the second the idea popped into her head. There was no way she was going to sit idly by while he made plans for her festival. And whatever ploy he was trying with a band...she wasn't having any of it.

"He said to call." Archer eyed her suspiciously and shrugged. "Besides, I thought you said you weren't hiring a—"

"I know what I said. And I don't know what the hell he's up to, but it can't be good. I have to get to the bottom of it." Sam stuffed the paper into her back pocket and grabbed her keys. "Preston, I'm sorry but I have to take care of this and—"

"Meet me for dinner."

"Sorry, what?" Her mind was already on the task of dealing with Trent and the festival; she couldn't deal with Preston on top of it all.

"Yes," Preston said. "I know you're busy and—"

"I don't think that's going to happen, Preston." The words surprised her. She'd never turned him down and if he'd come in and offered her the same invitation a month ago, she knew her answer would have been different. But that was before.

"Pardon?"

"Oh, I think you heard her." Archer looked as if he was ready to give her a high five or do a ridiculous fist pump or something. Sam ignored him.

"It's not going to happen, Preston. I've moved on."

The words where out of her mouth before she could think about their impact.

"What?"

"With who?" Both men spoke at the same time.

Sam looked at Archer, whose mouth was agape, his eyebrows wiggling comically. She smacked him in the chest. "It doesn't matter."

"It's that guy from the other day, isn't it?"

"Who? Trent?"

Her face heated at the mention of his name, and she wasn't the only one who noticed. Archer laughed and she shot a glare in his direction.

"Sam, we can make this work." He reached out for her arm, but she sidestepped him just in time. "We're made for each other and I know you feel the same way. We belong together. We always have."

For a brief moment, she let herself consider what he was saying. But even if he hadn't broken her heart on more than one occasion in the past, or treated her like she was a disposable townie, she knew in that moment that it was never going to happen with him. "I'm sorry you feel that way." She didn't bother to soften her tone. "Because I just don't feel the same way. But I'm sure you'll find someone someday."

Before he could say anything else, she turned and headed

out through the bar. Sam didn't let herself feel bad for letting him down. Not even when she heard Archer's laughter and Preston muttering, "Oh, shut up." There was nothing between them, and they both knew it. But with him officially out of the picture, Sam suddenly felt lighter, freer, and more...available.

Chapter Five

SHE DIDN'T WANT to like the Springs. And admittedly, she hadn't been up the mountain road that led to the resort since they'd first broken ground on the monstrosity that she was sure to find as she rounded the corner of the steep mountain road. The resort was only a few minutes out of town, but the twisty road made it feel much more secluded than it was.

Sam drove her beat-up truck past a simple sign with The Springs written on it, went around one more bend, and then there it was.

It wasn't ostentatious or gaudy or any of the things she pictured it to be. Instead, what she saw would have taken her breath away if she was the kind of girl to have her breath taken away by things as simple as well-designed buildings. It was much smaller than she'd expected. Maybe only eight stories at the highest point, but the majority of the building was low and consisted of glass and rock, as if it was trying to blend into the mountainside, which it almost accomplished.

She pulled her truck up the circular drive and was greeted by an attendee. To his credit, he didn't even blink at her rusty pick-up.

"Good afternoon," the man said when Sam opened her door.

"Um, hi. I just need to find a place to park."

"Are you staying with us at the Springs?"

"No." The word shot out of her mouth. She swallowed and tried again, a little softer. "No. I'm just visiting.I didn't think you were open."

"Not officially." The man smiled. "Enjoy your visit. I'll park your vehicle for you." He handed Sam a tag and waited for her to step down from the cab. She'd never experienced a valet before. Especially in the town of Cedar Springs. The whole thing was a bit over-the-top. But, with no other options, Sam snatched up her purse and hopped down.

"Thank you," she mumbled and turned toward the main building.

Enormous glass doors greeted her, flanked on either side by water. She looked closer and it appeared to be a stream that wound around the building and under the slight bridge she stood on. The whole effect was so subtle, she would have missed it if it weren't for the spotlights that pointed up from the water onto the walls of the building.

Sam tried not to be impressed, but when she walked through the doors into the main lobby, that plan went out the window. There was no way she couldn't be impressed with the beautiful space. The glass and rock theme carried over inside, as well as the water. A perfect balance of modern and rustic, the entire effect was serene and stunning all at the same time.

She tried not to gawk, but it was pointless as she took in every detail. Every negative emotion she'd felt on her way up the mountain disappeared as the tranquil space worked its magic on her.

"Can I help you?"

The sweet voice shocked her, and Sam took a stumbling step back. She caught herself moments before she smashed into a potted plant. She looked up into the kind eyes of a pretty woman.

"Hi," the woman said. "I'm Carmen. Is there something I can do for you?"

To Carmen's credit, her gaze didn't even flicker as she undoubtedly must have taken in Sam's jeans and t-shirt. Definitely not spa or luxury resort wear. There was no judgment on her face, only kindness.

"I was just...I'm here to..." Sam stopped herself, took a deep breath and internally chastised herself. She was being ridiculous. It's not as if she'd just set foot into the Royal Palace. It was a hotel, for goodness' sake. And it wasn't even open yet. She tugged on her t-shirt, smoothed her hair back off her face and tried again. "Hi. My name is Samantha Burke. I need to speak with Trent Harrison."

Carmen's face flashed with something Sam could have sworn was humor, and her lip flicked up into a tiny smile before it was replaced by the woman's professionalism. "Absolutely. Come with me, and I'll make sure he's in."

Sam followed the other woman across the tiled lobby floor, trying to discreetly look around. The actual lobby was fairly small and intimate, almost as if they were trying to create a sense of privacy.

"Just give me one second and I'll make sure he's in his office."

Sam nodded and tried not to eavesdrop as Carmen spoke into a phone to someone who was obviously Trent's assistant. Of course he'd have an assistant. He probably was the type of guy who used his assistant to pick up his dry-cleaning and run all his errands as well. Not sure where that thought came from, Sam tried to control her growing antagonism—admittedly probably fueled more by the desire she felt in her gut every time she thought of him rather than irritation.

"Trent's in his office." Carmen drew Sam's attention.

"Trent?"

Both women turned to see another very good-looking and somewhat familiar-looking man walking toward them.

"Dylan." Carmen held her arm out and the man slipped in for a hug and a kiss on the cheek that looked a lot more intimate than was likely intended. "This is Sam Burke. She's here to see Trent."

"Hello." Dylan turned smoothly and held out his hand. His smile was genuine and completely disarming. "You're the young lady of the infamous Grizzly Paw, aren't you?" He shook her hand.

"I am." Sam narrowed her eyes suspiciously.

"Word gets around," Dylan said with an easy laugh. "It's a small town and Trent could not stop talking about—"

Dylan rubbed his arm where Carmen had just smacked him. "Your burgers. He couldn't stop talking about how great the burger was."

Sam wasn't stupid; she knew there was more than was being said, but she also wasn't in the mood to investigate. Besides, despite the fact that she wanted to hate everything about the Springs, so far it'd been quite the opposite, and that included the people. Carmen and Dylan both seemed to be genuinely nice people. The kind of people she could see herself hanging out with.

"Why don't I take you to see my brother? I was just heading that way anyway."

Sam stared at him. Of course. That's why he looked so familiar. And now that she knew it, she could easily see the similarities between Trent and his brother. But there were differences, too. Where Trent was fair, Dylan was dark. And Dylan was slightly taller, and maybe a bit broader in the shoulders. But there was something else…Sam knew exactly what it was that set the brothers apart. Trent oozed sexuality. Just being in his presence made her stomach clench, and a heat grow deep in her belly. She'd never felt anything like it before, and who was she kidding, she hadn't been able to get that particular feeling out of her head.

"Thank you," she said after a moment. She sincerely hoped the heat she was feeling in her body didn't show on her face. "I forgot you were brothers." Dylan raised his eyebrow and with a wink, she added, "Word gets around."

They left Carmen at the front desk, and Dylan led her to the back of the lobby, where the room opened up, leading to an expansive corridor. One entire wall was glass, so it almost felt as if they were walking right in the mountains, instead of in a posh resort. The other wall was one enormous wall of water, slowly trickling into an unseen pool. The sun coming in through the windows lit up the space, glittering off the water. The result was magical.

Sam stopped in her tracks and stared all around her.

"I keep forgetting how amazing this is." Dylan stopped next to her. "It's pretty spectacular, isn't it?"

"I don't think there's a word," she breathed.

"Trent will be glad to hear you like it." She looked at him. "It was his idea to bring the outside, in."

She couldn't find any words, so Sam continued to walk. Pretty soon, Dylan had led her out of the great hall and into a small circular space with a number of doors branching off.

"Here we are. It was nice to meet you, Sam." Dylan reached for one of the door handles. "I hope to see you again."

"Thank you. Same here," she said, and meant it.

A moment later, the door opened, and Trent stood in front of her. That raw energy she'd felt from him the first time they'd met hit her full force. She hated the way her body betrayed her with this man who she really didn't want to like. And it wasn't just that he represented everything she hated—no, Dylan did too. But it was different with Trent. More personal. She pulled her shoulders back. She wasn't going to let him get to her.

"Samantha."

But the moment he said her name as if it were a wish, her resolve melted.

"Trent." She managed to push his name from her throat.

"I'll leave you two alone." Dylan chuckled and then he disappeared, not that Sam had noticed he was still standing next to her. She hadn't.

"You got my message."

It wasn't a question, which was good because Sam wasn't about to answer him. He moved away from the doorway and with a sweep of his arm, gestured her into his space. She hesitated. Of course, she'd come to talk to him, to confront him and to find out what he was trying to prove. But now that she actually stood in front of him, so close she could smell the scent of him—all fresh and clean, and so very male—it no longer seemed as if being alone in his office would be a good idea.

She took a step inside.

FOR A MOMENT, Trent didn't think she was going to come in. He would have held his breath if it wouldn't have made him look so completely out of control. And just because simply being in the presence of the woman did things to his sanity that he couldn't seem to either control or explain, he had enough sense to know that holding his breath would most definitely not help the situation.

To his relief, she did enter his office and before she could change her mind, he slipped around and closed the door with a click. He couldn't be sure whether he did it more to lock her in, in case she decided to flee, or for the privacy the door would afford. Probably both.

"I was hoping you'd come," he said after a second.

She swallowed hard and he watched the flutter of her

eyelids as she struggled to regain her control. Clearly he had a similar effect on her as well. The thought made his groin ache, and he moved behind the desk, needing a little distance between them.

"Sit. Please."

She scooted the high backed leather chair a little farther away from him. And as if the action and the distance between them allowed her the opportunity to think clearly, she opened her pretty mouth. "Archer told me just to call you back."

"Smart man."

She tipped her head. "You didn't want me to come?"

"On the contrary. I wanted nothing more."

Every word he spoke was true. He did want to see her again. The thought of her had kept him awake at night and occupied almost every waking moment besides that. From the moment he'd laid eyes on her, he knew there was something more about her. Something he'd never experienced from a woman before. Something he had to have.

"I need to get to the bottom of this, Trent," she said. He had to force himself to focus on her words and not the way her chest heaved when she spoke. "I don't know what you're trying to do by getting involved with the festival, but you need to butt out. It's mine. And outsiders have no place at the festival, let alone having a hand at organizing it."

"I'm hardly an outsider." He walked to a small table next to the window where he had a jug of water and a few glasses. He needed a distraction, preferably one that would cool him down. "I don't think I'd consider a major business owner of Cedar Springs an outsider."

"Well, you are."

He glanced back at her direction, but she wasn't looking at him. Her arms were crossed and her lips set in a firm line. He was definitely having an effect on her and it was far from the one he wanted.

"Water?"

"What?" Her head spun in his direction.

"Water." He held up a glass. "Would you like some? It comes directly from the glacier. It's fantastic."

"I've had glacier water."

"So you know how amazing it is." He grinned and held the glass up again.

"I'm fine, thank you." Crossing her arms a little tighter, which had the fortunate effect of squeezing her breasts up, she turned away from him.

"It wouldn't kill you to be nice to me, you know?"

That got her attention, and she hopped up from her chair, her cheeks blazing. "Nice to you?" She stepped closer. "You want me to be nicer to you? How about you stop trying to ruin my life and just leave me alone?"

"Whoa." Trent put the glass of water down. "That's what you think I'm doing?" Although he was definitely not trying to ruin her life, he also knew that since Samantha had managed to get under his skin, he was most certainly not going to be leaving her alone. "You think I'm trying to ruin your life?"

She put her hands on her hips, which only managed to pull her t-shirt tighter across her chest. Trent's groin twitched in response. Did she have no idea what kind of effect she had on men at all?

"What else would you be doing?" she snapped. "First you build this…" she waved her arm in the air searching for a word, finally settling on, "monstrosity."

Monstrosity? The Springs was a lot of things, but it was far from a monstrosity.

"And then you push your way into my best friend and her daughter's lives, and don't even get me started about the way you're totally ruining this town. And now this? What do you think you're up to, bringing a band in for the festival? The festival is mine. Cedar Springs is mine, and you need to…you need to leave."

Despite the fact that she was yelling at him, or maybe it was because of that fact, he closed the distance between them and put his hands on her shoulders. She shivered under his touch but didn't push him away.

"You don't want me to leave."

"Yes." Her breath hitched. "I do."

"No you don't." And to prove his point, he bent and let his lips meet hers. She stiffened, but still didn't push him away. With great restraint, he moved as slowly as he could make himself. He threaded one hand behind her head to the base of her ponytail and pulled her in while his mouth worked hers. Seconds later, he was rewarded by her yielding, as all at once Samantha softened and gave in to him.

She tasted sweet, almost like honey. A direct contradiction of her strong attitude, the juxtaposition was intoxicating. In a perfect world, he would have kissed her all day, because holding her in his arms and tasting her sweetness was like nothing he'd ever experienced before. But it wasn't a perfect world, and if he didn't stop, he wouldn't be held responsible for where his actions would lead him next.

Reluctantly and with his entire body straining with objection, Trent pulled away, gently sucking on her bottom lip as he did. Samantha immediately bit her lip, but instead of lowering her gaze or pushing away from him, her eyes locked on his. He still held her close. It took all the willpower he could muster to not pull her back into him again and show her exactly what being in her presence did to him.

"I'm not going to apologize for that." He may have released her lips, but his arms were still wrapped firmly around her, reluctant to let her go.

"I didn't ask you to." Samantha's eyes challenged him, and he met their challenge with one of his own.

"Have dinner with me tonight."

A flicker of something crossed her face. And Trent was so certain she'd say yes, especially after that kiss that was loaded with all kinds of feelings, that when a moment later she said no, it took all the control he had to keep from throwing her over his shoulder like a caveman and hauling her out then and there.

"We both need to eat."

"I have a date." Her words sent a shock through his system so that he dropped his arms and took a step back.

"Another time, then." In an effort to regain control of both himself and the conversation, he turned away and returned to his glass of water. He drank slowly while he stared out the window.

When he turned around, Samantha had moved safely out of reach and crossed her arms across her chest again, effectively putting up the walls around her once more. "I still want you to butt out of the festival," she said. "That didn't change anything."

She was wrong. That kiss had changed everything.

SAM FORCED herself to keep her eyes on Trent, when all she really wanted to do was look away. Just long enough to take a breath and get some sort of grip on herself. She'd lied. That kiss had changed everything. But there was no way she was going to let him know that.

"I want to help," Trent said. She forced herself to focus on what he was saying, reminding herself of why she'd come to see him in the first place. "I know a band. And I can get them to—"

"I don't need or want your band," she shot back. "The Grizzly Paw will host, just as we always have."

He nodded. "I heard it was quite the party last year. Sounds like you pulled out all the stops. Like maybe you had something to prove."

His words hit close. Way too close, but there was no way she was going to let him know that. Sam swallowed hard. "I don't have anything to prove. I'm not new to town. It seems to me that it's you and your big fancy hotel that has something to prove." She didn't mean to sound like a bitch, but he brought something out in her. And it was more than the heat that she was still trying to cool down from after that kiss.

"That's right." He crossed the floor toward her, and Sam had to fight the urge to flee. It was dangerous if they were too close. The kiss they'd shared had been hot. Hotter than hot and she wouldn't apologize for it. But even if every nerve ending in her body was screaming at her to grab him and go for round two, she knew enough to know it was a bad idea. Kissing Trent Harrison would not lead to good. Hell, it would only lead to confusion, trouble, and…she couldn't think. He was too close. She inhaled, trying to ignore the scent of him that spiraled through her senses. "Didn't you call it a…" He tapped his finger on his chin before he smiled and continued. "Oh yes, a monstrosity. That was the word you chose, wasn't it?"

"I…okay…well, maybe it—"

"But this is your first time here, isn't it?"

She nodded, because there was nothing else she could do. His proximity was clouding her thoughts, making it difficult to focus on a coherent response.

"Well then, how about I show you around and after I've given you a proper tour, you can decide if you still think the Springs is a monstrosity." His eyebrows lifted as he spoke the last word, as if he already knew she didn't really believe what she'd said earlier. Of course she didn't. The Springs was beautiful, even if she hated to admit it.

"Okay," she said after a moment. "But only the highlights."

Trent grinned like a lion who'd just cornered his prey. "Oh, they're all highlights." He reached toward her, and Sam instinctively closed her eyes, waiting for the touch of his lips again. "And when we're finished, if you agree that the Springs is beautiful, you'll let me arrange the band. If not, I'll leave you alone."

She knew it was a terrible deal, especially because she already knew she'd lost and the thought of him leaving her alone caused a certain pain in her chest. "Agreed," she heard herself say.

He smiled. His eyes never left hers as he reached behind him and clicked the door open. "After you," he said. Sam couldn't be sure but she could have sworn there was a hint of self-satisfaction in his voice, as if he already knew he'd won.

Sam turned and led the way out of his office and into the relative safety of a more public space.

True to his word, Trent showed Sam the highlights of his resort hotel and it didn't take long for him to convince her that the Springs was anything but a monstrosity. Especially as she never actually believed it in the first place. The entire place was amazing. And after a few minutes, it became clear that Sam wasn't going to find any fault with anything except for the fact that it existed at all.

"This is what I really want to show you." Trent guided her through the lobby and toward what she assumed would be another impressive glass corridor. "I've been saving the best part for last."

Sam walked past him, careful to avoid contact as she stepped into the space. She immediately stopped short and sucked in a breath.

"Well? What do you think?"

She turned to him, aware her mouth was hanging open before turning back to the sight in front of her. "These are the hot pools?" Sam walked toward the large glass windows. Much like the other enormous hall, this one also had a wall of glass—only instead of looking out over the rugged landscape outside, this window looked onto what was a large pool area with a variety of small pools. The area was constructed in such a way to allow the people in the hallway to see the hot springs, but the steam coming from the water acted as a privacy screen, creating a misty, almost mystical atmosphere.

"They are." Trent led her farther down the corridor. "At least, these are the public ones. We have a more private area, as well as the outdoor pools and of course the natural pools as well."

"Natural?"

"You do know all the hot pools are actually filled from naturally occurring hot spring water that comes out of the earth, don't you? I mean, you've lived here your—"

"I know that." And she did. That was why the springs had always been so amazing. It was a naturally occurring phenomenon that the water bubbled out of the earth, creating pools. When they were teenagers, Sam and her friends would visit in the night, often with alcohol they'd snuck from their parents' liquor cabinets. It didn't seem to matter that the springs were on private property. Or maybe it did. It just made it more exciting. It was also part of the reason Sam hated Trent and his resort. They'd taken everything that was special about one of her favorite places and commercialized it. She turned to look out the window again, mostly so she wouldn't have to look at him. Her body still needed time to return to normal. "I just didn't realize you kept any of the natural pools."

"I made sure of it." His voice was soft in her ear, his breath hot on her cheek as he came up behind her. Every nerve ending in her body fired. "The first time I saw them, I knew they were special."

She nodded.

"I can show you, if you like?"

"I know where they are." She forced her voice to sound as normal as possible, but with every word she spoke, she knew she was failing miserably. What was it about the man that made her completely lose her senses? Before she let herself get too comfortable, she slipped to the side and away from the heat his body was emitting. "Do you have a regular swimming pool, too?"

His lips twitched up in a smile. "Of course. Did you want to go for a swim?"

"I'm more of a lake girl myself." Sam flipped her hair behind her shoulders and grabbed her phone from her back pocket.

"You swim in it? Isn't it a glacier-fed lake?"

She looked up from her messages, which were mostly Archer demanding information on why she would turn down the offer of a band for the festival. She pushed the button to ignore the messages. "Chicken?" she asked Trent.

"Of a little cold water? Never."

"Good. We should go sometime then." The offer was out of her mouth before she realized what she'd done. She was supposed to be putting distance between them, not creating opportunities to get wet and half naked with him. Oh God. The thought of Trent without a shirt on, glistening with droplets of water was almost enough to send her right back into his strong arms.

"I'd like that. Maybe after we talk about the band for the festival?"

And there it was. The reminder of why she couldn't like the man. "We have nothing to talk about."

"Let me do this," he implored. "I know people and no," he held up a hand to ward off the comment that was on her lips, "that wasn't meant to sound arrogant. But I do know a band who owes me a favor. Jacked Crackers. They'd come and—"

"Jacked Crackers?" They were a rock/folk group that was currently dominating every radio station. Why would they want to come to Cedar Springs? She asked as much.

"I went to school with the lead singer, Axel. He's a buddy and I'll trade him a couple nights' stay in one of the suites. He loves to play smaller gigs."

"We won't be able to afford it. The Jacked Crackers are huge."

He shrugged casually. "It wouldn't cost you a cent."

That caught her attention.

"What do you mean, it wouldn't cost a cent? Nothing's free."

"This would be."

She doubted that very much. Even if there was no price tag on the band, there were other costs. Like her pride.

"I know you need help." His voice softened. "And I really want to do this for the people of Cedar Springs. We can have a dance floor outside, and…"

"How do you know I need help?"

Trent opened his mouth and closed it again before he licked his lips. "Just a hunch."

He knew. She didn't know how he knew, but he knew and at that moment Sam knew she had a choice. Accept his help and give the town and her friends the festival they deserved, or lock in and let everyone suffer because of her pride and what-ever misguided feelings she was having toward her unexpected savior. "Okay. The festival is on June twenty-first in the green behind the Grizzly Paw. There'll be a small stage, but make sure they know it's a small-town thing."

"Done." He could barely contain his grin. He looked like a schoolboy who just won the spelling bee. "It's going to be great. You'll see. Besides," he added with a wink, "now you won't have to make up excuses to come see me."

Chapter Six

TRENT FELT like celebrating as he saw Samantha out to her truck. Although he was almost positive it was a premature celebration, it was a celebration nonetheless. She'd agreed to the band. And maybe it wasn't the war, but he'd definitely won the battle. And that was something. More than something.

Now, if he could have convinced Samantha to stay and have dinner with him, instead of rushing off to the date she said she had—if that's what it really was—he would have had a real cause for celebration. But it was for the best. The last thing he needed was a date or God forbid, a relationship. A kiss was one thing, but dinner, or anything more…no. He couldn't go there. And Samantha wasn't the type of woman to have a one-night stand with. No. It was best she'd turned him down.

He waited until her truck left the lot and drove out of view before he headed back inside. He was almost across the marble floored lobby when a voice stopped him.

"Brother."

He turned to see his brother Dylan walk toward him with a grin spread across his face. Trent, matching his little brother's smile, strode across the floor to meet him. "What's up, little brother? Is there something we need to discuss?"

Trent asked the question despite the fact that he was perfectly aware of the answer. And it wasn't a surprise when Dylan clamped his hand on his shoulder and squeezed. "Oh, I think we both know what we're going to talk about."

He had two choices. He could play dumb with his brother or he could play along and tell Dylan what he knew he wanted to hear. It wasn't a secret that he'd met Samantha, and there was no doubt he'd seen them together. If Dylan was half as observant as Trent gave him credit for, he would have definitely noticed the heat between them, which is undoubtedly why he was here talking to him at that moment. Trent didn't do relationships. He didn't pursue women and he definitely didn't invest any type of emotional energy in a woman. Which is why it was absolutely insane that every single moment he spent with Samantha made him feel like all his nerves were on fire. It shouldn't be happening. He was too professional for that. Way too in control.

"I don't know what you're talking about." He slipped away from his brother and together they walked through the lobby in the direction of their offices. "Things are looking good around here, aren't they? Almost ready for the opening."

"Don't try to change the subject."

"Wouldn't dream of it."

Dylan shot him a look but didn't press the issue.

"She's cute," was all he said.

Trent nodded. It's not like he could disagree. She was cute. She was also hot in a feisty, he-needed-to-have-her-or-burst kind of way, but he wasn't going to tell his little brother that. Especially not after he'd almost single-handedly ruined Dylan's own happy ending with Carmen.

But that was in the past, and neither of them seemed to hold a grudge against the fact that he'd basically tried to sabotage their relationship from the get-go. Ultimately, it'd all worked out fine and that's all that mattered. The how and why of everything wasn't important.

"Really cute," Dylan pressed, and when Trent didn't take the bait, he added, "She seems to like you, too."

"Do you think so?"

A moment too late, Trent realized he'd fallen for it.

"I do," Dylan said. "And it seems my big brother also thinks so. Who is she?"

"I don't think…" There was no point in lying. "She owns the Grizzly Paw, the—"

"Pub in town."

Trent looked at his brother with a raised eyebrow.

"What?" Dylan held up his hands. "I know the local business. It's kind of our job to know the businesses of the town we're coming in to."

Trent's faced flamed and he looked at his feet while they walked through the hallway. Dylan was right. It was their business. Or at least, it should have been. He'd wasted too much time thinking he could come into Cedar Springs and make the resort its own separate entity. He'd been naive and arrogant. Meeting Samantha had taught him that.

"Yeah," Trent mumbled after a minute. "We should know what's going on with the town, which is why I agreed to help out with the summer solstice festival."

Dylan stopped in his tracks and it took Trent a moment to realize his brother wasn't walking next to him. When he noticed a second later, he paused and looked over his shoulder. "What?" Trent wasn't stupid. He knew exactly what. And he didn't wait around to hear about it firsthand.

When Dylan caught up to him, he grabbed his shoulder and spun his big brother around. "Tell me you didn't commit the Springs to something we can't deliver on."

Trent shrugged. He wouldn't tell him anything if he didn't

want to hear it. Besides, this was his department. Dylan was in charge of operations and getting the entire resort off the ground. He didn't need a majority vote to commit his time and effort to a few local promotional efforts.

He shrugged.

"Trent."

He pulled away from his brother's grip, suddenly irritated by the intrusion. "It's good," he said, in an effort to retain some form of peace. "I'm going to get Jacked Crackers to come and play. It's not a big deal and I'm looking out for the reputation of the hotel with the locals."

"The hotel?" his brother challenged. "Or yourself?"

Trent's eyes narrowed and he took a deep breath to maintain his calm. "I don't think you meant to ask that question."

"I did." Dylan squared up. For all Trent's talk about his little brother, there wasn't much discernible difference between their size. But for what Trent lost in physical size difference, he made up for with the natural big brother threat.

"Are you sure?" Trent challenged.

Dylan took a breath and Trent could tell his little brother was squaring up for a fight. It wouldn't be an easy win. It never was with two stubborn bastards in the family.

"You might want to—"

"Hey." Carmen interrupted with a smooth hand on each man's shoulders. "I think that's enough testosterone from both of you this afternoon."

Trent took a step back and looked between them. Dylan immediately turned to Carmen with nothing but love in his eyes. It didn't matter what the woman said; he melted like a pile of goo for her. It was disgusting, really. Or at least, he used to think so. If he was the kind of man who wanted a relationship—and he wasn't—he might want something like the two of them shared. But as it was, he wasn't built for relationships.

That had been proved years earlier with Britt, his high school girlfriend.

He'd thought he'd been in love. And maybe he was, but he was too young and too stupid to see clearly. His father had always warned both of them that women were no good, and they'd only get in the way of their success. But he wouldn't listen, even when Trent's dad threatened to disinherit him. What he shared with Britt was real; it was stronger than his dad's threats. Or so he thought. When his dad couldn't scare Trent into breaking up with Britt, all it took was a check with the right amount of zeros for her to decide it wasn't love after all.

His father had been right. If that was love, he didn't need it. If he wanted to be successful, he couldn't be tied down to a woman. It was one or the other. Business or women. And he'd made that decision a long time ago. Samantha was nothing more than a scratch he needed to itch. That was it.

"I'm fine." Trent shook her off.

He walked to the window wall. The mountains were coming more to life every day with their summer flowers and greenery. He should get outside. He should go for a walk. When was the last time he went out? He let his brain flip back through the last weeks and couldn't remember, which was enough of a sign for him.

"I'm going for a walk," he announced, totally unaware of the looks the other two were giving him.

"No." It was Carmen who reached out and slipped her arm through his. She pulled him in close and held him to her side. "I think we should talk about this."

Out of reflex, he shook his head. "I don't think we—"

"She's right, brother. What's going on?"

Trent stopped and looked at Dylan. He'd always been so professional and analytical before he'd hooked up with Carmen. Although Trent was doing his best to be happy that

73

his little brother had found love despite the odds played to them from their upbringing, he needed all three of them to have their heads in the game as far as business was concerned. They were too close to the opening of the resort to afford any screw-ups and if Dylan and Carmen were more worried about their love life—or his for that matter—it wouldn't do anyone any good.

"I don't think that matters right now," Trent said after a moment of reflection. "I think that what matters now is that we do everything it takes to get the Springs off to the best start we can." He removed Carmen's arm from his and before either of them could press the issue, he pushed out a side door into the summer afternoon sun.

BY THE TIME Sam drove down the mountain and pulled up to her small house, just down the street from the Grizzly Paw, she knew she should change her clothes and head back to the pub. But all Sam really wanted to do was run a hot bath, pour herself a glass of wine and replay that kiss with Trent. Okay, that wasn't the only thing she wanted to do. But going back to the Springs to find Trent and finishing what they'd started didn't seem to be a very reasonable option.

Before she could make a decision about the evening either way, a knock sounded on the door. She was halfway across the living room floor when the door opened and Archer came bursting in.

"What are you—"

"Wanted to make sure you're okay."

"I'm fine." She shot him a look and shook her head.

"Good," he said. "You're not going out with him."

For a flash of a second, Sam thought he was talking about Trent. He was the enemy, or at least, she thought he was, but that was before. "Wait." She shook her head to focus on the moment. "Who?"

"Preston." Archer watched her carefully. "Who did you think I was talking about?"

"Oh, him. Of course I'm not. I'm over him. Big time."

"Really?"

"Really." She turned and walked through the house into her kitchen, where she grabbed a bottle of wine from the rack. "Do you want a glass?"

"I actually believe you. Something's different." Archer came in behind her, pulled out a chair and sat backwards on it. His arms rested on the back. "Do you have a beer?"

"It's wine or nothing."

"Wine."

She pulled the cork and poured them each a glass. "Why are you here? Shouldn't you be at the bar?"

"Kylie and the girls have it under control. It's not that busy."

"It should be busier," she said as a reflex and jumped up on the counter.

"When the new hotel opens, things will pick up." Archer took a tentative sip of his wine, shrugged and took a bigger gulp.

"Do you really think that? Or is that something you're telling me so I don't worry?" She really wanted to know. For the last few months, Archer had continually told her not to worry. But that was easy for him to say when she was the one who saw the bank account and the money or lack thereof in the account. The way she looked at it, the Springs was going to be ruining everything, not saving it. The resort was changing the entire feel of the town. It would never be the same once it opened. But it was beautiful and maybe Archer was right; maybe it would bring more people into town and therefore more people to the bar. She just didn't know what to think anymore.

"Hello?" Archer's voice brought her back to the moment. "Are you in there?"

"Sorry. I was just thinking."

"About what? Or should I say, who?"

She sighed and rolled her eyes. "I don't know what you're talking about."

"Sammie, who knows you better than anyone?"

"Beth." She hid her smile.

"Besides Beth?"

"Okay, okay."

Archer held out his glass and they clinked on it, both of them drinking deep.

"But there's nothing to tell."

"Uh huh." He drained his glass. "What's going on with Harrison?"

She almost choked on her wine. "What makes you think there's anything going on with Trent?"

"Maybe the way you just turned bright red and almost spat your wine out all over the kitchen." He shrugged. "But that's just a hunch."

There was no way she was going to talk about her love life or whatever it was that was going on with Trent—not with Archer. Nothing good had ever come from getting him involved in her personal relationships. He was way too protective of her to see that she actually might want to settle down and have a real relationship with someone because she couldn't be alone forever, making the Paw her entire life. The reality of her thoughts slammed into her. Is that what she really wanted? A relationship? With Trent?

Sam hopped off the counter and put her glass down. She was getting ahead of herself, way ahead. They'd shared a kiss, nothing more. The fact that that particular kiss had her toes curling in her shoes, and had sparked a burning low in her belly that she couldn't seem to forget, wasn't important. Or was it?

"Sammie?"

"I'm not talking about it with you," she answered, her back to him. "Even if there was something going on, which there isn't, you'd find some way to disapprove or make sure he stayed away from me and..." She hung her head, and bit her lip hard to keep the sudden flood of emotion back. What was wrong with her? She never cried. Especially not over some messed-up version of what she thought she wanted out of her life.

Archer's arm slid over her shoulders and pulled her close. Reflexively, she turned in to him and let him hug her. It felt good to be consoled, even if she didn't know why she was upset. "I'm not going to ruin anything for you," Archer said. "I'd never do anything that would hurt you." His hand rubbed circles on her back and she sniffed into his chest, aware that the tears she didn't want to be crying soaked his shirt. "I only want you to be happy, little sis."

She smiled and pulled up so she could look at his face at the use of the nickname he hadn't used in years. "That's better," Archer said. He used his thumb to wipe her cheeks. "It's not worth crying over."

She sniffed again and pushed away to grab a tissue. "I don't cry."

"I know." He raised his eyebrows and sat back.

"It's stupid."

"Not if it's making you upset." His words hit home. "The last time I saw you cry is when—"

"They died." She finished the sentence because she knew exactly when it was. When her brother crashed the car he was driving with their mother in the passenger seat, killing them both instantly, Sam's entire world changed in that moment. No longer was it in the plans for her to go to college. It was all she could do to graduate from high school. Her father turned to alcohol, drowning his problems in the bottom of bottle after bottle, not only drinking away the profits of the Grizzly Paw but effectively destroying the only livelihood they had left. It had been up to eighteen-year-old Samantha to put her own plans on hold and keep everything running. It also meant she needed to steel herself against her new reality. A strategy that had served her well, even through her break-up with Preston. Everything had been fine, until that moment.

"Yes," Archer said softly. "So whatever has you so upset right now, I know it's serious. And Sam, I don't mean to sabotage anything, I just…Preston…"

"Stop." She held up her hand. "You've never been anything but wonderful to me." She felt the pressure of the tears building again, and blinked hard to keep them at bay. "Don't think for a minute that I've ever felt any differently."

"But you want more?"

For the last eight years, Sam could honestly have said no to that question. Everything she wanted was in the town of Cedar Springs, and running the Grizzly Paw had been fulfilling. Even when Preston left her and broke her heart only to play with it again at will, it hadn't crushed her because what she'd had was enough. And deep down, she knew he wasn't the one. She looked at Archer, who was waiting for his answer. Slowly she nodded. "Yes." Her voice was barely more than a whisper. "I think I do. I just don't know what that looks like right now."

"It doesn't have to look like anything right now."

Did she hear him right? That didn't even make sense. She told him as much.

"I'm serious, Sam. You don't have to decide what your future looks like. Not right now, anyway. You have time. The key is knowing you want something different. You can figure the rest out later."

Her reflex was to protest, but she stopped herself. He was

right. In his own crazy way, Archer was actually making sense. Just knowing she wanted something more was enough. And just because she came to the realization while being totally and unexplainably attracted to Trent Harrison didn't mean anything. Did it?

"So what do I do in the meantime?"

"Enjoy yourself." He shrugged as if it was just that easy. "You're young and you're beautiful. Why does it need to be more complicated?"

Instead of answering him right away, she poured herself another glass of wine and refilled his as well. "I'm not really the one-night stand type." She handed him the glass, which he took with a silent cheers.

"I didn't say that." He wiggled his eyebrows. "But if you wanted to be…"

All it took was a dirty look to shut him up, but Sam couldn't help but think of the option. It might not be terrible to…no. She couldn't do that. Especially not with Trent.

"You're thinking about it, aren't you?"

"No."

"Yes you are," Archer teased. "Don't worry, I'll never tell."

Sam sipped her wine, letting the rich taste roll around her mouth before she swallowed it. "You never know. Maybe I'll think about it."

"I'll drink to that." Archer held his glass up and Sam met it with a clink and a smile. "I mean it, Sam. You don't have to take life so seriously. Have a little fun."

Chapter Seven

TWO DAYS LATER, Trent still couldn't get the woman out of his head. It had to stop. For days he'd walked around in a fog, remembering the way her soft lips yielded to his. The way her whole body melted into him and the soft moans of pleasure that escaped her. It was all he could do to keep from driving down the mountain to the Grizzly Paw to pull her into his arms and see what kind of noises she'd make when he pressed her up against the wall and showed her exactly how crazy she was making him.

It had to stop. For at least the fifth time that morning, Trent ran his hands through his hair and tried once again to focus on the papers in front of him and put her out of his head. He had work to do. They were set to open the Springs the day after the solstice festival. It would be the first official day of summer and the perfect time to orchestrate the quiet launch he had planned.

The Braxtons were worried that without a big grand opening, the Springs wouldn't make enough of a splash to register in the market. But Trent was counting on the very fact that they weren't having one to differentiate them among their competition. The Springs was positioned to be a world-class resort that offered a soothing escape for guests. And a large party celebrating that fact would be in direct contrast to what they were trying to accomplish.

But the solstice was only five days away, which meant all the loose ends needed to be tied up and the final preparations completed, and there was no more time to waste. Although it wasn't a full guest list, they'd managed to book up at least half of the rooms for the first week and Carmen told him registrations were coming in every day. With any luck at all, the summer would be a success to set them up for the rest of the year and Les Braxton could settle down and trust that his investment was in capable hands.

That wasn't the only thing he wanted in capable hands. His mind shifted in an instant, the image of Samantha's soft curves under his palms as he stroked down her—

"Trent."

Carmen's voice as she entered his office without knocking shocked him out of his daydream and just in time, too, because if he entertained his fantasies of Samantha much longer, he would need to find some kind of release. He was getting sick of going to his suite alone every night.

"What's up?" He straightened in his chair and tried to look as if he'd been busy working instead of fantasizing about the local pub owner.

"There's a little girl here who said she's working for me today." Carmen gave him a look that told him in no uncertain terms that he better know what she was talking about or there might be hell to pay.

"That's Jules."

"Jules?"

"She's going to be working for you for a bit."

"Is that right?" Carmen crossed her arms and Trent did his

best not to laugh. "And have you bothered to check into the child labor laws? Because she looks to be about ten."

"Eleven, actually."

"Okay. Eleven. And what exactly am I supposed to have an eleven-year-old do at a luxury resort for adults?"

Trent crossed his arms over the papers on his desk, happy for a break from the subject that was distracting him from work. He relaxed into his chair. "I'm sure you can find a few things for her. Have her fold towels on the pool deck or maybe —I have the perfect idea. I'll have her help out with the festival."

"The festival?"

"It's a summer solstice festival that the town throws every year."

"I know what it is."

"Then why did you ask?" Trent pushed his chair out and stood. It was fun to tease Carmen, especially when she was wired so tightly with the opening around the corner.

Carmen dropped her arms and sighed in frustration. "I meant, why are you involved in the festival? It's Sam Burke, isn't it?"

"You told me to build a relationship with the townspeople and do something nice for them. That's what I'm doing." He opened the office door and held it open. "Come on. Let's go find Jules."

She shook her head, but led the way out to the hallway. "That's not exactly what I meant," she said. "And I definitely didn't mean you had to build that type of relationship with the locals," she said after a minute. "But if that's what floats your—"

"It's not like that." He spoke the words, but was glad that they were walking and Carmen couldn't see his face. They'd known each other long enough that she'd easily be able to see there was more to it than what he was saying; he just wasn't ready to have that discussion. Particularly not with his brother's girlfriend. "They were in need of some entertainment for the festival, and I knew I could help. Besides that, it will be a good launching pad for the Springs. It's the day before our grand opening."

"You mean the non-event that we're calling a grand opening?"

Trent glared at her. "We decided it was best to have a quiet open."

"I know." She slapped his arm. "I'm teasing. But that doesn't solve the problem of Jules."

"I'm a problem?"

At the same moment, Trent and Carmen froze and turned to see Jules staring up at them. For all her bravado, her lower lip quivered and Trent thought she might cry.

"'Cause I'm not," Jules said.

Trent squatted down and took her hand. "No." He forced her to look him in the eyes. "You are definitely not a problem. I was just talking to Carmen about how you were going to help us solve our problems around here."

She stared at him without blinking, as if she was trying to figure out if he was full of it or not. Finally she blinked and nodded. "Okay. I can help. What are we doing?"

With a big smile, Trent stood up and gestured for her to follow him. "Come on. I have a very important project for you, and I think you're the perfect person for the job."

Together they walked down the hallway and out of the corner of his eye, he saw Carmen smile and shake her head before she joined them.

WITH HER CLIPBOARD IN HAND, Sam left her office and made her way through the kitchen. She grabbed a bun from the basket Archer had set out as she went past.

"That's not lunch," he called after her.

"It's lunch enough."

"Get back here."

There was no point arguing with him, and she knew it, but she also knew she had far too many things on her list to be able to sit down and eat a meal. "Archer, I don't have—"

"You don't have time not to have a good lunch."

"That doesn't even make sense." She laughed because although it really didn't make sense, she knew he meant well. And the knowledge that she wasn't going to have a chance to eat again until much later, combined with the mouth-watering smell of whatever it was Archer had cooking away in the big pot on the top of the stove, convinced her that she had time to have lunch. "Fine, I'll eat. But I only have a few minutes."

"It won't take any time at all. Go sit down. I'll bring it right out."

Sam did what she was told and pushed through the swinging door into the bar. Her top waitress—and only employee she trusted almost as much as Archer—Kylie was filling two glasses of draft.

"How are things looking out here, Kylie?"

"About the same as they usually are." She winked and expertly flipped the tap up as she put the glasses on her tray and hoisted them up to her shoulder. "Actually, for a Wednesday afternoon, it's busier than usual. There's a whole group of guys who said they're working up the mountain on the resort."

"Really?" Sam arched her neck to subtly check out the men. "That's…"

"Great?"

"Yeah." She nodded her head distractedly. "It's great.

But…why now? They've been building that place for months and we've barely seen anyone."

"I don't know," Kylie said. "But I'm not complaining. This is the second day they've come in and I sure like their tips."

Sam watched as she sashayed her hips across the room. Just enough of her midriff showed under her Grizzly Paw t-shirt and she had to smile. Sam knew exactly why Kylie was getting the tips. She was a great waitress and the fact that she was young and cute didn't hurt one bit. She shook her head while she watched Kylie place the beers on the table, and take the orders with an easy flirt.

"I'm glad they came in."

Sam spun around at the voice. Trent stood only inches away from where she sat on the bar stool. Her heart rate instantly increased to a rapid beat that she hoped he didn't notice. "What are you doing here?"

"Hello to you, too." He slid onto the stool next to her and all at once Sam wished he'd picked somewhere else to sit. His sheer proximity was making her heart beat fast, and her hands itch with the urge to wrap themselves around him and pull him into her. She'd thought of little else since their shared kiss the other day, and she wanted more than anything to enjoy a repeat performance. But that couldn't happen. Especially not in the middle of her bar.

"Sorry," she mumbled. "I just didn't expect you here."

"Why not?" He smiled and if Sam was less of a woman, she would have melted at the devilish grin. As it was, she was having a hard time behaving normally in his presence. "After all, I needed to go over the details of the festival with you. Jacked Crackers needs to be sure of the stage size and overall space they're dealing with. They're used to playing larger venues, so if they need to make any adjustments it's better that we know that ahead of time considering they won't be in town long."

"Oh my goodness." Sam slapped her hand to her forehead. "I didn't even think of where they'd stay. We have a few rooms upstairs, but they haven't been rented out in ages and I could probably clean them up, but—"

"I got it."

"Pardon?"

Trent spun so he faced her. His hand reached out and squeezed her thigh in what she assumed was an effort to calm her down, but all it did was send her spinning in a million other directions.

"I've got it," Trent said. "They can stay at the Springs. We'll be officially opening the day after the festival, so the rooms will be ready and with them as some of the first guests, hopefully they can help spread the word about the place. We have plans to offer them a full range of services as well so they can—and…I'm boring you."

"No," she answered truthfully. "You're not. I'm just starting to realize why you're doing what you're doing." She twisted in her seat so her back was facing him.

"Pardon?" When his hand wrapped around her shoulder, Sam had to fight the urge to lean back into him. His touch felt so good and it would be so easy to let him hold her up, even if she now realized his motives were purely for his own purposes. He hadn't wanted to help her at all. But didn't she know that? He was a business man. Of course he wasn't trying to save her festival. It was all about his resort and how they could publicize it.

A wave of laughter from the corner caught her attention and she turned to see the group of workers flirting with Kylie as she placed their lunch orders in front of them.

"Looks like you have some satisfied customers," Trent said. When she still didn't turn to look at him, Trent's hand slid up her back, and under the wave of hair that cascaded down her back. Thrills shot through her, but still she fought the urge to let it show how much he affected her.

"What do you need to know for the band?" Sam shot up so she stood next to the bar, and just out of reach of Trent and his touch that was threatening to make her come completely undone.

He smiled, as if he held a secret, but didn't say anything about her abruptness. Instead, he crossed his arms. "Actually, that's not really why I'm here today."

"Then why are you here?"

She didn't mean it to sound rude, but the moment the words were out of her mouth, she wished she could take them back. Something about him prickled at her. Even as the very presence of him was turning her on and causing her stomach to do weird flips and things, she wanted him to leave her alone. It was a push and pull that she couldn't quite explain.

Before he could answer, the kitchen door swung open and Archer appeared. He held a tray with a bowl of steaming soup and a fresh bun on it. "Trent." He greeted the other man. "Can I get you anything?" He slid the fragrant bowl in front of Sam; it was all she could do not to immediately dig in. She was hungrier than she'd thought and Archer was right—she needed to eat.

"No, thanks, man. I can't stay today."

Her stomach flipped with disappointment at Trent's words.

"I just stopped by to let Samantha know about her assistant."

Assistant? Sam's ears twitched, suddenly paying attention.

"She'll help you out with all the last-minute details and help you with any final preparations."

Sam dropped her spoon. "I don't need an assistant."

"Everyone needs a little help."

"I don't."

"Let me help you, Samantha."

Sam flicked her gaze between Trent and Archer, looking for even the slightest bit of support. The traitor simply shrugged and smiled. "I think I have some stuff to do in the back," he mumbled and made his escape.

Chicken, she thought. But she didn't need his help, anyway, and she definitely didn't need an assistant. Besides that, in a budget of zero, there was no money to pay a helper.

"Trent, I don't need—"

"I'm told she's really good with decorations. Paper pom flowers are her specialty. Not that I know what those are." He shrugged and for a moment looked so innocent and relaxed that Sam was instantly attracted to him again. She had to stop that. It wasn't healthy for her to be constantly turned on by a man she was never going to be with.

"What do you mean she's good at pom flowers?"

"You know what they are?"

She remembered some large tissue paper things hanging from the ceiling at Beth's house right after they moved in. They were in a medley of bright colors and were actually quite pretty. "I have an idea," she said.

"Good. Because I'm told she's the best," Trent held up his fingers in air quotes, "pom flower maker in town."

A smile lit Sam from inside. "Jules," she said.

"Oh, so you know her?"

Trent winked and as if they'd practiced it for hours, Jules walked through the front door, her arms loaded down with a pile of tissue paper in a variety of bright colors. Sam rushed to alleviate the girl of her burden.

"What are you doing here, kiddo?"

"Isn't it great?" Jules's big eyes were wide with the hopeful expectation that Sam wouldn't crush her excitement. "I'm working for Mr. Harrison now and my first job is to help you with the festival."

She raised her eyebrow. "Yes." Sam glanced at Trent, who

watched the scene unfold with humor in his eyes. "I heard you'd made friends with Trent."

"Mom told you."

Sam nodded.

"Did she tell you I was working at the Springs?"

"She may have mentioned it." Sam picked up a piece of red tissue and folded it absentmindedly between her fingers. "But I don't understand why you're here if you're supposed to be working at the Springs. Don't you have towels to fold and flowers to water and things like that before the guests start knocking down the door?"

"I thought Jules would be put to good use helping you this week," Trent said. "I know you have a lot on your plate and this way you don't have to worry about the decorations. Jules is in complete control. She has a budget and she's been specifically instructed to stay out of your way, so you can worry about all the other things you might have to worry about."

Sam glared at him but she couldn't seem to find fault in his proposal. Not only would there be some decorations, when all she'd thought of was turning on the Christmas lights she hadn't gotten around to taking down, but it would make Jules happy, which in turn would make Beth happy. And at that moment, Sam couldn't find anything wrong with that.

"I think it's great," she said. "I hate decorating, so if you can take care of that for me, you'd be a real lifesaver."

The little girl's eyes lit up. "Really?"

"Of course. But I expect you to work hard. I'm not going to cut you any slack just because you're you."

Jules nodded solemnly. She looked around, taking in the space around her. Technically she wasn't supposed to be inside, but because the Grizzly Paw was one of the only places to eat in town, most people overlooked that small detail. At least until after the dinner hour. Jules was no stranger to the pub. "I have a lot of work to do here," she said after a moment.

Sam tried not to giggle at her seriousness. She nodded in agreement. "You do. But don't worry too much about the decorations in here. Let's focus on the outside."

"Yes," Jules said, all business. "I'll go check it out."

After the girl left, Sam was all too aware of Trent's presence next to her.

"I hope it's okay," he said. "I know you don't want any help, but…"

"No. It's fine." Determined to focus on something besides Trent's proximity to her, she picked up the bun on her soup and ripped off a small piece. "But about the budget for decorations…"

"I've got it. Please don't worry about it."

The last thing Sam wanted was to be indebted to him for something else, but she couldn't see how a few poms would cost much and if it made Jules happy…

"I should let you get back to your lunch."

Disappointment washed through her again. What was it about this man? He drove her crazy with his presumptions and the way he pushed his way into her life and her town, but whenever he wasn't around, there was nothing she wanted more than to see him. And kiss him.

The thought flashed through her so quickly it made her cheeks flame. Her first instinct was to keep her head down, so he wouldn't notice. But why did it matter? Discarding the bun on the plate, she looked up and took a chance. "Why don't you stay?"

He was busy with his resort opening in less than a week and he had far more important things to do than to sit in a pub and have lunch with her. She knew that and the practical side of her brain told her not to get her hopes up that he might actually want to spend time with her. But the other part of her brain, the part that had completely dominated every thought and feeling since they shared that kiss, wouldn't listen. And despite what Sam knew, she was still disappointed when he said, "I can't." He reached out and tucked a strand of hair behind her ear with a tenderness that sent sparks of desire shooting through her body. "It's just that I have—"

"You don't need to explain to me." She pulled back, just far enough so he couldn't touch her. She had no business feeling any of those things when clearly it wasn't the same for Trent. "I get it." She picked up her spoon and dug into her soup, which was quickly cooling.

"Samantha."

She didn't look at him. She couldn't. She'd taken a chance, albeit a small one, and it was easy to see where he stood. If he didn't have time, she certainly wasn't going to give any more of hers. She shoved a spoonful of soup in her mouth and if she hadn't been so preoccupied with the man standing next to her, she might have noticed how delicious it was.

"Look at me."

She took a big bite of the bun and kept her gaze focused on the bowl in front of her. She would not look at him; she wouldn't give him the satisfaction of knowing—

"Please."

She looked.

"I don't have time right now." His low voice was full of something Sam didn't recognize. Lust? Maybe. "But tomorrow?"

Her heart did a strange flipping, squeezy thing but she was determined not to let this man get to her. She couldn't afford any more hurt or expectations. Besides that, all she really wanted from him was another kiss. Nothing more and definitely not anything that required either one of them to make a commitment beyond the festival.

She smiled, making sure to look as unaffected as possible. "We'll see. Actually, I have plans for this afternoon anyway."

"Is that right?" He leaned up against the bar and gave her a look that made it very clear that he didn't believe her.

She put another spoonful of the soup in her mouth, and took her time swallowing before she said, "It's such a beautiful day I thought I'd go for a swim. You have to take advantage of these days when they come up. Before you know it, the summer season will start and things will be too busy." She was babbling and she knew it, but she couldn't make herself stop, so she shoved another bite of soup in her mouth.

"A swim, huh?"

She nodded.

"Is the offer still open?"

"What offer?"

"The other day, you told me we should go for a swim sometime."

Of course she'd said that, but she hadn't meant it. Had she? "I thought you didn't have time today?" She narrowed her eyes and watched carefully for his response.

He leaned in, resting on the bar, inches from her. "That was before."

"Before what?"

"Before swimming was on the table. I'm ready when you are."

THE WORDS WERE out of his mouth before he even realized what he'd agreed to. Swimming? In the lake? Never mind that the water was probably cold enough to freeze him on the spot, he had a to-do list a mile long and Dylan would kick his ass if he found out Trent had blown off work for swimming.

But it didn't matter. None of it did. He couldn't say no to her, not that she'd even asked him, but that was a small, unimportant detail. There was something about Samantha. Maybe it was the fact that she tried hard to ignore the heat between them? The key word was tried. Because Trent wasn't blind: he could see the way her skin pinked when he was near, the way her breathing got just a little bit faster. He noticed everything. Because he felt the exact same way.

He couldn't get her or the sweet heat of her mouth out of his head. He wanted more. Needed more. And wasn't that the real reason he found himself walking down the beach to where she was waiting?

He kicked his shoes off, leaving them by the grass, and tucked his socks inside before picking his way across the sand. Samantha was right—it was a beautiful day. The sun warmed his face and the sand beneath his feet. It almost felt like summer already. The water would be refreshing and a nice way for him to clear his head and get refocused for the rest of the day.

"Are you coming?" Samantha turned around and called to him before she faced the water again.

He had his mouth open to reply, when she pulled her t-shirt over her head and rendered him speechless. She was gorgeous. Her hair, released from the ever-present elastic, fell in dark waves over her bare shoulders. Recovering his senses, he jogged the rest of the way to where she was standing in nothing more than a red bikini top and her jeans.

"Where's your suit?"

Trent looked down at his black dress pants and buttoned up shirt. He hadn't thought of a suit.

She shrugged. "That's too bad." She smirked before turning her attention to the button of her jeans. Trent had to fight the urge to take care of the task for her. And when she slid the denim down her hips and shimmied out of her pants, leaving them in a pile at her feet, it was all he could do to keep his hands to himself.

She was delectable, with her body curving in all the right

places. Dangerous places that encouraged every dirty thought he'd ever had to flood his mind. He looked to the lake, and then back at Samantha. Suit or not, he was getting in the water with her.

"Who needs a suit?" Trent almost laughed out loud at the look of horror on her face.

"You can't…it's a…" Her gaze drifted down the length of him, and Trent could only imagine the dirty places her own mind was going. He'd like nothing more than to go there with her.

He slowly unbuttoned his shirt, and pulled it from his arms. He folded it and placed it next to her messy pile of clothes before looking at her. There was heat in her gaze as she checked him out, and Trent took his time, relishing the fact that he wasn't the only one affected.

"You can't skinny-dip." She finally found her words. "It's a public beach."

Trent raised his eyebrow and slid the leather of his belt through the buckle.

"Trent." Samantha put her hand on his before he could unbutton his pants. The heat of her hand had an immediate and very dramatic effect on him, and there was no way she could have missed it. She snatched her hand away and stared at him as a blush crept over her. "You…you can't."

"Relax." He attempted to apply the same advice to himself. "I'll swim in my shorts."

"Oh." Her face pinked further, the blush spreading to her chest, and dipping between her breast. "Of course." She dipped her head and before Trent could say anything else, Samantha ran into the water, where she pointed her arms over her head and dove gracefully beneath the surface.

He wasn't going to let her get away that easily. Grateful she was already in the water and couldn't see his very obvious arousal, Trent stripped his pants and ran to join her. He imitated her dive, only when he broke the surface, the air was sucked dramatically out of his lungs, leaving him breathless. When he surfaced, he struggled to regain his breath and composure.

"It's...it's...friggin' freezing!"

Her laughter rang out, and if he hadn't been experiencing some form of shock, he would have taken offense. A splash of water hit him in the face. He wiped his eyes and looked to the source. Her hair was slicked back, the water giving her an exotic quality that had Trent's body reacting once again, despite the frigid water.

"Don't be such a baby," Samantha said. "It's not that cold."

"You're crazy. It's like ice in here."

"If you don't want to swim, go back to the beach." She turned away from him and dove under before she surfaced and glided into easy, long strokes that took her away from him.

Hell no. There was no way he was getting out. Not when that exquisite water nymph was only a few feet away. Accepting her challenge, he dove under, kicking hard, and pursued her.

His years in swim club as a child paid off, and it wasn't long before he'd caught up with her. Before he could overthink it, he grabbed her slippery leg and pulled her back, using his strength to bring her close.

"What the—"

Trent brought his mouth to hers, kissing away her protests. He let his hand slide down her smooth back, resting on her buttocks and the tiny scrap of fabric between him and her skin. Just as she had the other day, Samantha's body responded to his kiss, and soon the temperature of the water was not an issue because there was more than enough heat between them.

Her hands gripped the hard muscles in his back and one slick leg wrapped around him, locking her to him. A primitive groan came from his throat and he pulled her up against him, hard. He let his free hand travel down her body and cup the swell of her breast before moving to the base of her head, deepening the kiss. He wanted her closer still. Needed her closer.

Damn, he needed a lot more than that. He'd never felt a need so deep and all-consuming with another woman.

Samantha was the one to break the kiss, pulling back so suddenly that Trent lost his grip on her, and she deftly turned and dove under the water, putting distance between them.

"You should probably go in," she said when she surfaced. "Before you freeze to death." She was far enough away that Trent couldn't read the look in her eyes, but not so far that he couldn't see her chest still rising and falling from the passion they'd just shared.

She was giving them an out. Things between them couldn't go any further and they both knew it. As much as every fiber of his body yearned to have her, Trent knew better. It was different with Samantha. More intense, more…real. And he knew enough to know he needed to stay far away from real. That wasn't his style.

"You're right." He ran his hands through his wet hair, slicking it back. "Besides, I should get back."

He didn't wait to see whether she would say anything more. He didn't think he'd be able to handle it if she did. As it was, it took all his focus and determination to turn and swim away from her.

DAMN THAT WOMAN.

Trent pushed down on the accelerator, and despite the fact that he knew he was going too fast for the mountain roads, he needed to put distance between him and Samantha quickly, before he turned his car around, barged back into her bar and showed her exactly how much he wanted to be with her. But he couldn't do that.

He pushed the car further and hugged the corner of the road, needing the release the speed gave him. He was too close to the line. Too close to caring about her and the incredibly sexy way she pretended not to want him, even though her body and her kisses screamed out the exact opposite. The way she tried to be tough when he knew there was a soft woman underneath that hard exterior who was yearning for escape.

The lights in his rearview mirror quashed his growing desire for the woman he'd left down the mountain.

"Shit."

Trent immediately slowed the car and as soon as he could find a safe place to pull over, he did so. There was no point dragging it out.

"License and registration."

Trent had them ready and he handed them over to the officer, who flicked his gaze between the cards and Trent.

"You're that resort guy," the officer, whose tag said Anderson, said. He didn't say it with disdain or anything else that would give Trent the idea he wasn't welcome. But given that the topic of the Springs resort was a hot-button issue with most of the townspeople, Trent thought it would be prudent to use caution.

"I am." He nodded. "Sorry about the speed," he said after a second. It was just as easy to get it out of the way. They both knew he'd been speeding; there was no point denying it.

"These roads are no place for showing off," Anderson said. "By the time you meet another vehicle, it's too late."

Trent nodded solemnly and waited for the officer to hand over his ticket, but to his surprise, Anderson handed his license and registration back. "Slow down, okay?"

"Thank you. I will." He turned to shove the cards back into his wallet, and when he straightened up, he expected the officer to be gone; instead, he was leaning against the car, his arm on the window.

"How are things going up there?" he asked. "You're getting ready to open?"

"Only a few days now. We're just putting the final touches on things. The official opening is the day after the festival," Trent said.

Anderson smacked his palm against the roof of the car. "Well, you're doing good things, Harrison. I know the people of Cedar Springs really value the business you're bringing in."

Trent smiled. At least one woman didn't share that sentiment, he thought. At least she hadn't, but maybe things were changing. "Thanks, man." He pushed thoughts of Samantha from his head. "Everyone's been really welcoming." It wasn't entirely true, but with any luck...

"I'll let you get back at it then. But slow down."

"Absolutely."

Trent waited until the officer got back into his patrol car before he eased back out onto the road, this time making sure he stayed well within the speed limit.

When he walked through the main doors, his agitation only increased. And not because of the almost speeding ticket he didn't get, but because of the damned woman he still couldn't get out of his head. Hooking up with Samantha, in any kind of way, would be nothing but trouble. What had his father always said about women? They were more trouble than they were worth and they always ended up costing you in the end. Somehow, Trent knew the cost would be higher than simply money if he got involved with Samantha. She obviously had a chip on her shoulder and the last thing Trent needed was a project. He didn't have the time or patience to convince her that he wasn't the enemy. But damned if he didn't want to try. All it would take would be another kiss, maybe a—Dammit.

He had to stop thinking of her. He kicked a tool bag that

was lying in the middle of the foyer. Kurt, his head maintenance man, looked up from the fountain he was working on.

"Trent?"

"Don't tell me that fountain is broken, too." Kurt had been
working overtime to get everything working in time, and even
as he came down on the man, he knew it wasn't fair but he
couldn't seem to stop himself. "These fountains should be
working by now."

"Sorry, Trent. I think it's a faulty pump." The other man
ignored his boss's mood. "It hasn't worked properly from the
get-go. We have more pumps in storage. I'll get it fixed."

"Good." Trent swallowed hard and tried to rein in his
mood a little. "What the hell is the problem with all the water,
anyway? If it's not one of them, it's another. And the whole
image of the resort is based on water. The features have to be
perfect."

"They will be. I'm going to figure it out," Kurt said.
"Everything will be fine by Sunday."

"It better be."

Kurt raised an eyebrow but wisely decided to get back to
work rather than add any more fuel to what looked like could
be a very explosive fire.

"You're not distracting our number-one handyman with
stupid requests again, are you, brother?" Dylan called from the
other side of the lobby. He smiled and made his way across the
marble floor to Trent.

"I'm just trying to make sure everything is perfect."

"It will be." Dylan turned to Kurt, who was packing up his
tools. "Room 302 has a light switch that isn't working. Can you
take a look at it?"

"Absolutely, boss. I'm on it." Kurt gave a quick look in
Trent's direction before making his escape.

"I need him to fix these fountains." Trent slapped his hand
against the side of the basin and stalked away toward the

pools. "The water is...dammit." He didn't trust himself in his current mood to be around people. He needed space.

But that didn't stop his brother from following him. "What's going on with you?"

"Nothing."

"Liar."

"I don't want to talk about it."

"She got to you." There was just a touch of humor in Dylan's voice that caused Trent to spin around and face his younger brother.

"I don't—"

"Save your breath, brother. You're totally and completely a mess for that woman."

Trent shook his head, but didn't bother objecting. There was no point. And Dylan would know the signs, considering he'd just recently fallen completely in love with a woman who had messed him up just as badly. The fact that Carmen and Dylan had managed to work through their initial rocky start actually gave Trent a glimmer of hope that there might be the possibility of a relationship with Samantha.

"No," Trent said more to himself than to deny his brother's accusation.

"Yup. You're screwed." Dylan laughed again. He didn't need to stick around and watch the obvious enjoyment his little brother was getting from the situation. He turned and pushed open the door that led to the gardens. "Hey," Dylan called.

Trent froze, halfway out the door. The laughter in Dylan's voice had been replaced by something else. He didn't turn around but he waited and listened.

"He was wrong, you know."

If he'd punched him, Dylan couldn't have impacted him more. Without having to say it, Trent knew exactly who Dylan was referring to. He squeezed his eyes shut against the flood of emotions he didn't want to feel and inhaled deeply. He struggled to keep it together and not let the impact of his brother's words show.

"Allowing yourself to feel something for a woman isn't a sign of weakness," Dylan continued, either unaware of Trent's internal struggle, or more likely, perfectly aware. "It's a sign of strength. Dad was wrong to tell us otherwise."

He couldn't stand there and listen to any more. Still he didn't turn around, but Trent shook his head hard in an effort to clear out his brother's words and walked away. As he turned the corner down the path that would lead him up the hill to the natural springs, he heard his brother call out after him.

"You deserve to be happy, Trent. Don't shut it off."

Trent pushed on, determined to leave everything behind him, especially the growing feeling that his brother might be right. That was the part that scared the hell out of him.

Chapter Eight

"WE WILL PUT the bar over here, and the tables behind it will have to be kept stocked with glasses. Close enough, but not too close that they'll be in the way." Sam walked the perimeter of the field where, in less than forty-eight hours, hundreds of people would be standing, enjoying the solstice festival. There was still so much to do, and even though she was just a kid, Jules had been a fabulous assistant.

"Do you have enough glasses?" Jules took notes in her clipboard.

"Oh no." Sam smiled. "Not real glasses. We'll use plastic cups. There should be enough left over from last year in the storage room. I do not trust my glasses out here with all those people."

"Of course." Jules nodded solemnly and scratched something else on the paper.

She was a sweet kid, even if she wanted everyone to think she was strong and independent. She reminded Sam so much of herself when she was young. And heck, even as an adult. There were pros and cons to a personality like that, she thought. It could be exhausting.

"Hey," Sam said. "You've been working really hard and I appreciate it so much, but don't you think you could use a break?"

A look of horror crossed the girl's face and she shook her head. "Oh no, Auntie Sam, I told Mr. Harrison I was going to do a job, and I'm going to do it."

"I know, kiddo. But it's okay to take a break." She rubbed Jules's shoulder. "I'll deal with the big, bad Mr. Harrison if he gives you any trouble." She tried to keep a straight face while Jules battled with herself.

"I don't—"

The sound of laughter and kids playing coming from the beach, only a few yards away, caught her attention. Sam watched her turn to see a group of boys and girls running and splashing into the lake.

"Go," Sam said.

Jules shook her head and looked down at her feet. "No. I don't know them. It's okay."

Sam put her arm around her best friend's daughter, a kid she loved like her own, and squeezed. "They're good kids. Why don't you go and introduce yourself, and offer them an ice cream. I have some treats in the kitchen."

"Really?"

Sam nodded. "Go." She waved her arm. "I've got this. And you can always help me later if you want."

She seemed to think about it for another second before she nodded and smiled. "Thanks, Auntie Sam. You're the best. Here." She handed Sam the clipboard and headed across the lawn to the beach.

Before getting back to work, Sam watched her for a moment. Beth would be so proud to see her daughter introduce herself so fearlessly. It had to be hard to start over in a new town, but Jules was handling it pretty well. And she was a good kid, she'd be okay.

"Please tell me you didn't fire her?"

Trent's voice sent shivers down her spine and she couldn't tell whether it was because he'd surprised her or whether it was simply his presence.

"Hardly." She turned to see him walk toward her. Dressed in jeans, slung low on his hips, and a simple t-shirt, he looked even more gorgeous than when he was in his more professional work clothes, if it was even possible. She swallowed hard, remembering the hard, bare chest she knew was under that shirt. "I sent her on a break. She needs to be a kid. Besides, I can handle this." She crossed her arms over her chest as he came to stand beside her.

"Is that right?"

"Absolutely."

"It looks to me like you could use a little help." His voice was low, suggestion laced through his words, and Sam's body responded instantly.

She turned to face him and almost knocked into him, he was standing so close. His hands reached out to steady her, and the heat on her skin filled her.

"Careful." His hands held her forearms, and he didn't show any immediate signs of letting go. "Are you okay?"

Sam nodded, not trusting herself to speak. There was something about him. Whenever he was close to her, she had to work extra hard to keep her walls up so she could stay in complete control. But he'd caught her unprepared and her defenses were down. At that moment, with him standing only inches away from her, his hands on her, Sam had no desire to put those walls back up. Instead, all she could think of was the way his mouth felt on hers, the way her body melted into his and the unmistakable, completely consuming way she wanted him. And what was it Archer had said? Why does it need to be more complicated? Why indeed?

Before she could change her mind or listen to the voices in

her head telling her to back away and get some distance, she closed the small space between them and kissed him. His lips felt just as good as she remembered. Better. And if he was surprised at her forwardness, it certainly didn't take long for him to get over his shock.

Trent's hands left her arms to slide into her hair. He tugged her head gently to one side, giving him access to her neck. A moan escaped her as he nibbled down the length of her neck and sucked softly on her collarbone before once again finding her lips.

The heat between them was unmistakable, and Sam wasn't going to pretend she didn't want him. Not when every fiber of her body screamed out for his touch, the pressure low in her belly building with every second that passed.

"I don't think—"

"Don't think," she quieted him.

"Yes ma'am." Trent grinned wickedly, his green eyes darkening with passion. With a wink, he lifted her by the buttocks. Sam wrapped her legs around his waist, slid her hands up through his hair and pulled his mouth back on hers. Damn, she wanted those lips everywhere all at once. And there was way too much clothing between them. Never mind the fact that they were standing in the middle of the back field where anyone could come across them.

As if he read her mind, Trent walked, which couldn't have been any easy feat with her legs wrapped around his waist. To help him out, Sam pulled herself away from his lips and concentrated on his neck instead. She left a trail of kisses and he shivered beneath her.

"You're going to be the death of me, woman."

"Or both of us, if you don't watch where you're walking." She returned to her task.

He growled in a way that only made her want to tear his shirt off. Sam surprised herself with how bad she wanted him, and the completely uncharacteristic way she was showing him that. She pushed the feelings of doubt from her head. Archer was right. She was young and beautiful and why wouldn't she have a little fun? Besides, sometimes sex was just that. Sex. There was no reason it had to be anything more.

She was so busy justifying her behavior while trying to control herself, she hadn't noticed they'd stopped moving until her back bumped up roughly against a wall. Her feet found the ground reluctantly.

"Can we get in here?"

Breathless, Sam turned around in his arms to see he'd taken her to the boathouse. Technically, it belonged to the town and housed the various canoes and tiny sailboats they used for lessons, but because it was so close to the Grizzly Paw, Sam was unofficially in charge of keeping an eye on it, which meant she knew where the key was. She glanced over her shoulder at Trent, who waited for her answer, a look of pure lust on his face. She could think of a lot nicer places to do whatever it was they were about to do, but none of them were handy. And if she was given too much time to think about it, there was no doubt she'd change her mind. His eyes bore into her, the passion in them unmistakable.

No. She was definitely not going to change her mind.

"I have a key," she said after a moment. Sliding away from him, she bent down and aware of the view she was giving him, took a little more time than was necessary to pull the key out from under the brick next to the door.

"Get up here." His voice was rough with need and his impatience made her grin to herself as he wrapped his hands around her waist and drew her up against him. There was no mistaking his need for her to get the door open, and feeling his hardness pressed up against her only fueled her own fire.

Sam slid the key into the lock and led the way into the musty building. It was dark, with only a stream of light coming in through a small high window. Not that it mattered. She had just enough light to see. And her eyes were very much on Trent and his broad shoulders.

"Nice place." He crossed the floor and gestured to the pile of sails she was leaning up against. "I've always wanted to learn how to sail. I just never had the opportunity."

"Is that right?"

"Maybe you can teach me sometime?"

"I don't know." She ran her hand along the top of a sail. "Do you think you'd be a good first mate?"

He ran his hand down her denim-clad leg and Sam had to work hard to control the shiver that threatened to overtake her. "I assumed I'd be the captain."

She laughed. "Oh no, darling. I'd definitely be the captain. If you could handle it."

He looked as if he was going to say something about that, but instead he changed tack. "Well, I'm certainly glad you had the key to this place."

"I like to be prepared." Her voice came out in a low, sexy timbre she didn't recognize as her own. That's what he did to her. What he'd done to her since the moment they'd met, but now...

"Do you?" He reached her and traced a finger down her neck, into the peak of cleavage her tight t-shirt afforded. The sparks his simple touch sent through her body threatened to consume her. "But are you prepared for this?"

HER TONGUE DARTED out between her lips, moistening them, and Trent almost lost what little control he had left. From the moment he came upon her in the field, he knew something was different. There was a shift with her, almost a heat that was radiating from her. He'd known it was only a matter of time before their attraction came to a head. He'd worry about the consequences of his choice later, because for the moment, he was more than ready to see exactly what Samantha was hiding under those tight little t-shirts she liked to wear.

The only question that remained: was she ready?

He traced his finger along the swell of her breast, barely holding himself back from tearing the fabric away completely, and waited for her answer. She held his gaze, her chocolate eyes looking almost black in the dim light, or was it because she was turned on? It didn't matter. They transfixed him either way.

"Absolutely." She answered him after what seemed like forever. It was all he needed. Without wasting another moment, he slid his palms down her body, stopping to trail his fingers over her ripe, firm breasts. But the fabric was too much. A barrier he no longer had patience for.

With a quick tug, he eased it over her head to expose the sexiest purple lace bra he'd ever seen. Or maybe it was what the bra was containing. Regardless, the sight of Samantha standing in front of him half naked, her hair tousled, and her lips already looking deliciously bruised from their kissing was enough to undo him.

"Damn," he muttered.

"My turn." She reached for his shirt, but he beat her to it, pulling it over his head.

Her eyes racked over him, the hungry look turning him on even more, if it were even possible.

"No fair." Samantha stuck out her lower lip in a very sexy pout. "It was my turn."

"I thought I'd help. You don't like what you see?"

"Oh, there's no question about that." For emphasis, she trailed her fingers over his broad chest and down to his belt buckle, where they paused. "But I don't like getting robbed out of what's mine."

"Is that right?"

She seemed to contemplate the situation for a moment before a wicked glint flashed in her eyes. Before Trent even realized he'd lost control over the situation, her fingers were deftly flicking open his belt buckle, and easing the leather aside. She paused before pushing the button of his jeans through the denim hole, and in that moment when Samantha looked up at him, her tongue darting out from between her lips in a move that was so unwittingly sexy, Trent knew he was in trouble.

The feisty beauty had gotten under his skin and he knew it, even if he had been trying to deny it. But he didn't have time for that. He didn't have time for a woman, not even Samantha, with her sharp edge and strong will that was just begging for the opportunity to be vulnerable.

Dammit. Not only did he want to spar with her, he wanted to take care of her, all at the same time. He was in unfamiliar territory with her. And that was a dangerous place to be. Especially for a man who was used to keeping his personal conquests distinctly separate from every other part of his life.

Samantha eased his jeans and boxers down over his hips in one incredibly sexy and sensual move. He drew in a gasp when her mouth found him. He laced his hands through her hair and gave himself over to the feeling of her warm mouth on him and let his body take over when his brain could no longer capable to make the decisions.

Just this one time. That was it, he told himself as a groan escaped his lips. Just enough to scratch the itch that had been festering from the moment he'd walked into the bar and laid eyes on her. One time, he promised himself. That was it. Then he would have to get this woman out of his head.

Done thinking for the time being, he knew he had to regain control over the situation, and soon. Trent reached down, and pulled Samantha to her feet. The satisfied grin on her face told him she knew exactly what she did to him. But the heave in her chest and the way her breasts rose up and down with the passion she herself was barely containing told Trent he had the exact same effect.

———

SAMANTHA COULD HARDLY BELIEVE HERSELF. Never before had she behaved so wantonly, not even with Preston. Trent did something to her that she couldn't even begin to explain. Just being in his presence, never mind in all his naked magnificence—and it was magnificent—caused her to behave in ways she couldn't wrap her head around. She was way too in control and responsible to have a quickie in the boathouse.

But at that moment, looking at him in the dim light, the need in his eyes more than evident, she didn't need an explanation. She simply needed him.

Thankfully, Trent must have felt the exact same way as he reached for her. He slid a finger into the waistband of her jeans and tugged her toward him before quickly gaining access into the jeans. He slipped them down, his palms taking their time as they caressed her curves all the way down her legs.

Sam stepped out of her pants and in the next moment, Trent lifted her and as if she weighed absolutely nothing, he placed her on the pile of folded sails and climbed over her, shielding her entirely with his body. A shiver ran through her, as she stared up at him, but not because she was cold. Far from it. Her body felt as if it was going to explode from the heat coming off her.

"You're so beautiful," Trent said. "I just want to look at you." His eyes drank in her body as his fingers began their journey under the lace of her bra, pushing it down to reveal her breasts. Her nipples immediately hardened, yearning for his touch.

But instead of giving her the relief she craved, Trent continued his torturous travel, across the plane of her belly, to the waistband of her panties. For one terrible moment, she thought he might move right past, but no.

Mercifully, his fingers slipped under her panties, pushing the lacy fabric down over her hips. His fingers found the wet heat between her legs at the same time his lips crushed hers, swallowing her cry of pleasure. It took all her concentration to keep control as he explored her with one hand, causing the pressure in her core to build to an almost intolerable peak.

"Trent." She pulled her mouth away from his. "I...I..."

"I know." His voice matched hers. When he removed his touch, she didn't know whether to cry out in frustration or relief. What she did know was the time for messing around was through. She needed him. Now.

He leaned over the side of the sails, rustling in his jeans before producing a condom from his pocket. All Sam heard was the tearing of the foil. She squeezed her eyes in the anticipation, and she didn't have to wait long before he was there, stretching her and filling her—and it felt oh so good. A moan escaped her mouth and she wrapped her legs around his waist, drawing him in further.

He felt good. Better than good.

Every motion hit all her buttons, and it wasn't long before she felt the familiar build in her belly, stronger this time, demanding release.

Samantha ran her hands down his smooth, hard back, gripping his buttocks, urging him on. A call he answered readily. He felt so good, she never wanted the moment to end, but at the same time, her body had other ideas as it yearned and reached for the orgasm that Sam knew was right there.

There might have been a chance to ward it off a bit longer, but when Trent lifted his head, looked straight into her eyes and said, "God, you feel fantastic," and lowered his mouth to hers and kissed her with a heat and tenderness that belied the passion being created by their bodies, Sam's muscles tightened around him and she completely lost herself as she came undone around him.

WHEN SHE'D LET herself go completely, Trent almost lost it on the spot. Using all the restraint he could muster, he held off on his own release only long enough to watch her beautiful face as she gave herself up to ecstasy. Her expression and total giving of herself was enough to set him off, and he joined her in his own shattering orgasm.

When his senses returned to him, Trent rolled to the side and pulled Samantha with him so she was lying with her head on his chest. Her hair, tousled from their romp, spread over his chest and tickled him in a pleasant way. The sexy vixen of only moments ago was replaced with yet another side of the woman he hadn't seen yet. There was so much to her, it was as if he was always discovering something completely new about her. It was fascinating and very intriguing.

He lifted his hand and stroked her head, letting his hand trail down her back so he could pull her closer into his embrace. As if their coupling hadn't been enough, the need to be close to her, touching her had only increased.

Dammit. The thought flew through his head. It was supposed to be a scratch. That was it. Just enough to satisfy the itch he felt every time he saw her. Nothing more. He didn't want a relationship with her. Not with anyone. That whole idea of love and commitment might work for Dylan, but that wasn't in his future.

Yet he'd just considered the L word.

He tensed. His hand froze on her back and he knew the exact moment Samantha felt it too. She stiffened in his embrace but despite whatever turmoil was going on in his head, he wasn't ready to let her go. In fact, at that moment, he couldn't be sure he'd ever be ready to let her go.

Forcing himself to relax and shut off his mind so he could enjoy the moment, he continued rubbing her back, but it was too late. The mood was broken.

Samantha shifted and wiggled away from him leaving behind a cold spot where the heat of her had been.

"In a hurry?" He propped himself up on his elbow, trying really hard to come across as casual and unaffected, even though what he really wanted to do was grab her and pull her back on top of him to show her exactly what her presence did to him.

"I have to…this was…I should go." She wouldn't make eye contact with him. Hell, she wouldn't even turn in his direction. Instead, he watched, unsure of what to do while she scooped up her jeans, tugging them over her legs, not bothering to locate her panties.

"Samantha…" What was he going to say? He had no idea. All he knew was he didn't want her to go. Even if it had been in a boathouse, sex with her had been…intense was the only word he could think of. But logically, of course she had to leave. Hell, if he was thinking straight, which he so clearly was not, he should be hightailing it out of there, too. After all, he'd told himself it would only be once, and by the frantic way she was moving around the boathouse, that's all their coupling had meant to her, too.

Suddenly feeling very exposed, Trent hopped off the stack of sails and grabbed his jeans, pulling them on right as she located her t-shirt.

He felt a pang of regret as the cotton slid over her luscious breasts. They'd fit in his hands absolutely perfectly, never mind the way she'd responded to his touch on her. No. He shook his head and forced himself to focus on the moment, which was rapidly slipping out of his control.

Her face was impossible to read as she swept her hair up into a ponytail.

"No." He grabbed her hand before she could slip the elastic around her hair. "Leave it down. It's beautiful."

To his surprise, she dropped her hand and let her tousled hair fall around her shoulders. But he still didn't release her. With his free hand, he cupped her cheek and traced his thumb across her soft skin. When she sank into his touch and closed her eyes, he asked, "What are you rushing back to? Didn't I give you an assistant to take care of the details?"

"Shit. Jules." Her eyes sprang open and she tried to jerk away from him, but Trent held her arm and pulled her against his chest, holding her against his bare skin.

"Not so fast." Before she could protest, and he knew she would, he kissed her deeply and thoroughly to give not only her, but also himself, something to remember their boathouse rendezvous with.

When she finally pulled away, there was an unreadable expression on her face, and for a split second, he was worried she might cry. But then her face changed, and the tough Samantha he'd come to know was back. "I trust you can find your own way out?"

He nodded, even though it was clear she wasn't looking for an answer.

"Good." She sucked her bottom lip into her mouth and nibbled on the corner in a way that was so completely sexy, Trent had to shove his hands in his back pockets to keep from grabbing her again. The woman was out-of-control desirable. Even more so because she didn't seem to have any idea of what she did to him. "I guess I should..." She gestured to the door.

"Yeah." He nodded again. "I guess you should." He wanted to

take the words back and tell her that she shouldn't go. That they should stay there in the musty boathouse and hide for a little while longer. But he didn't. That would be encouraging something he couldn't follow through on. And that would only lead to trouble.

"Okay." She nodded. "I'll see you—"

"At the festival. The band has the details. They'll check in with you by two tomorrow."

"Great."

The awkwardness between them pained him. Samantha had already turned to leave so she didn't see him step forward and reach out to her. And she was already out the door, walking away from him when he let his arm drop. She was gone.

***

WHAT HAD SHE DONE? It was totally unlike her to give in to such ridiculous urges. Sam quickly glanced around as she put as much distance between her and the boathouse, and Trent, as possible.

Jules was still down at the lake with the other kids. They were close to the boathouse—too close. Would they have heard anything? Seen anything?

"Oh God."

She ran her hands through her hair, pulling it back from her face. She was such an idiot to think she could have a quickie with a man who made her tremble just by looking at her. Or a quickie with anyone, for that matter. Damn Archer and his stupid advice. But it was done. She couldn't turn back time and take it back.

And she wouldn't even if she could. Sam knew that in her bones. Even if it had been a mistake, sex with Trent was like nothing she'd ever experienced before. There was a connection between them. She could see it in the way he looked at her, in the way he—

"No," she chastised herself. "No more." She had to stop because if she didn't, she'd be running right back into the boathouse and into his—

"No more what?"

Sam jumped and would have screamed if it wasn't her best friend standing next to her. She hadn't even seen her coming across the lawn toward her. "Don't sneak up on me like that."

Beth laughed and rolled her eyes. "I hardly snuck up on you. I was right in front of you." She waved in the direction she'd come from. "You look a bit…preoccupied," Beth finished with a raise of her eyebrow.

"I am." Sam glanced back toward the boathouse, hoping the move was subtle, and hoping even more that Trent didn't choose that moment to leave. Especially if he didn't have his shirt on yet. She shook her head clear of the thought of his hard, smooth chest. She had to focus. "Come on." She grabbed Beth's arm, spun her around and headed toward the bar. "Did you come to help?"

"I came to pick up Jules, actually. Where is she?"

"She's down at the beach. I pointed out some kids for her to hang out with."

"And she did?" Beth stopped short, causing Sam to jar her arm. She released her friend and rubbed at it.

"She did. It's good for her."

Beth spun to see if she could catch a glimpse of her daughter hanging out with kids her own age. "That's great. She looks…happy."

"She is." Sam took Beth's arm again and walked. "We should go." The kids were skipping rocks right beside the boathouse. If they stood and watched much longer, there was no doubt Beth would get an eyeful of Trent. He had to come out sooner or later.

"What's your hurry anyway?" Her best friend eyed her, suspiciously, but walked with her. Her friend knew her too well, and unless she wanted to out herself, which she didn't, there was no other way around it.

"It's the festival." It wasn't totally a lie. "It's got me all worked up."

"Oh, really?" She batted her eyes innocently. "And I suppose this tousled look you've got going on here, along with that very gorgeous man who happens to be my boss who I just saw sneaking out of the boathouse, has nothing to do with getting you all worked up."

Sam stopped in front of the Grizzly Paw and stared at her friend. "What are you—"

"Don't even try to deny it." Beth smiled and fluffed Sam's hair. "You have 'I just had wild passionate sex' written all over you."

Sam shook her head away from Beth and headed up the stairs without bothering to respond. She went straight to the bar and poured herself a shot of whiskey.

"That bad, huh?" Beth caught up with her and plopped herself down on a stool, leaning on her elbow.

"Yes. I mean, no." She raised the glass. "I mean, I don't know."

Beth's hand reached out and gently brought the shot glass down. "Spill."

There was nothing to spill, but only because Sam couldn't sort through the swirl of feelings herself. But Beth waited for an answer. "It was amazing," she said, her voice quiet. The idea of whiskey had lost its appeal, so she pushed it away. "I can't even explain it but it was…"

"What?"

She released a sigh and searched for the right word. "It was like he knew me. Like, really knew me." She waved her sentimentality away with a huff and straightened her shoulders. "It's stupid. I'm being such a girl about it."

"You are a girl."

"But not like this. It was supposed to be a one-time thing. Just to get him out of my head, you know?"

"I don't. But that doesn't mean anything." Beth shrugged and Sam was reminded that her friend was a single mom, and she probably shouldn't be talking about random sex with someone who was probably too busy to even think about sex. "Seriously." Beth leaned forward on her elbows in rapt attention. "Tell me. I need to live vicariously through you. And I have a feeling this is going to be good."

"What's going to be good?" Archer appeared from the kitchen, a towel slung over his shoulder.

There was no way she was going to talk about it with Archer. Especially because it was his fault she was feeling whatever it was that she was feeling in the first place. If she hadn't listened to him and just kept ignoring Trent and how he made her feel, she wouldn't be standing there contemplating how exactly she was going to be able to see him again without wanting to drag him right back into bed. And that was not okay.

"Well?" Archer looked between the two women, but Sam kept her mouth firmly shut. Beth broke the silence.

"Sam was just about to tell me about sex with Trent and why it has her all twisted up in knots."

She tossed a paper coaster at her supposed best friend, which had the not so dramatic effect of falling flat in front of her.

"So you went for it?" Archer asked. "I can't believe it."

"Neither can I."

"No, I mean, I can't believe you took my advice." Archer nodded in self-satisfaction. "After all these years, finally something rubbed off."

"And it had to be this." The room was too hot. She tugged her hair back into a messy ponytail. It didn't matter if Trent liked it down; in fact, maybe that was the point. She needed to clear him from her head. "Of all the stupid advice you've given me, I had to listen to that."

Eyeing the shot of whiskey, he picked it up and quickly tossed it back, earning a glare from Sam. "It wasn't stupid. You had sex, didn't you?"

"I don't think I need to answer that question."

"I'm still waiting for details." Beth leaned back and crossed her arms over her chest.

They both ignored her. "Then mission accomplished," Archer said. "Like I said, you're young and beautiful. What's the harm?"

"Especially when there's so much heat between you," Beth chimed in.

Her face burned, remembering just how much heat there'd been. But it was more than that. It was the way he looked at her, and caressed her back, not wanting her to go.

"Why are you so upset?" Archer continued. "It's just sex."

"That's just it." Sam shook her head and looked up at her friends, unshed tears blurring their faces in her vision. "I don't think that's all it was."

Chapter Nine

TRENT LOOKED at his watch for at least the dozenth time. Only eleven in the morning. Way too early to go down to the festival. Heck, the festival wouldn't even start for another six hours or so, and with the band organized and set to arrive around two, there was nothing for him to do. Except wait. And pretend to work when all he really wanted to do was see Samantha. Besides, things weren't really going to start up until the sun started to set.

He stared at the papers in front of him. Carmen had brought in the latest bookings an hour earlier, and he liked what he saw. Some well-placed ads in the health and lifestyle section of some of the top newspapers in the United States were obviously working. The Springs was just far enough away in Canada to be exotic, but close enough to keep traveling expenses down. Besides, people were willing to pay for the healing powers of the natural hot spring water, especially when it was offered up in an elegant and comfortable atmosphere. And that's exactly what he had to offer. The Braxtons would be happy to see the numbers. In fact, there was no point waiting to tell them the news.

It was the perfect distraction to get his mind off Samantha and the way she'd moved underneath him, responding to every touch, every—enough. With determination, Trent punched in the numbers to his direct line and lifted the receiver waiting for Sam Braxton, the patriarch of the family, to pick up. It would probably be easier if he skipped over Les and went straight to the top.

"Harrison." The man's booming voice traveled over the line. "I was just thinking about you."

"And I, you." Trent smiled at his easy lie. The truth was, the Braxtons were good investors. They kept their nose out of the general operations, for the most part anyway. But their working relationship was a good one, and Trent liked and respected both of them, even if they did get in his way sometimes. "I have some good news for you."

"There's nothing I like better. Except maybe a single malt scotch and a beautiful woman."

"I think you'll like my news better." Trent chuckled and forced his mind away from one very specific beautiful woman. "How about the fact that for the first three months of operation, the Springs is on target to see almost eighty percent booking?"

"Eighty?"

He heard the hesitation in the other man's voice. "That's above industry standard, Braxton. And that's just the projected number. The way the bookings are coming in, I wouldn't be surprised to see that number go up by the end of the month. All in all, things are looking really good."

"And you boys are on track for opening tomorrow?"

Tomorrow. Wow, that had snuck up. Especially since his primary focus had been on Samantha.

"Of course." He tried to sound more confident then he felt. "Dylan's taking care of most of the last-minute details, but I have no doubt it will be perfect."

"I agree," Sam said. "I've never had anything but the utmost confidence in you both."

Really? Trent shook his head, happy they were speaking over the phone and the other man couldn't see him rolling his eyes. It wasn't long ago they'd had a conversation about building trust within the community and how they'd better get their numbers up. Trent shook his head and smiled. It didn't matter.

"And you'll be happy to know the Springs is playing a pivotal role in the town solstice festival tonight," he couldn't resist adding. "We've provided the band and of course most of the staff will be in attendance to show support."

"Sounds great. I wish I could be there but I know you'll handle everything."

"Yes sir, I will."

"Good. Now stop wasting your time talking to me and go take care of something."

Trent smiled as he hung up and his mind immediately went over his mental to-do list. But the temptation to blow it off was strong. Especially because all he really wanted to do was find Samantha. But she'd be busy with her own stuff, and the festival was important to her. He needed to leave her alone to get her work done.

But that was all he was going to leave her alone for. The decision had hit him sometime in the middle of the night. He may not know what it was with Samantha, but he knew what it wasn't. It wasn't a one-time thing. She was definitely not the type of woman to have a casual fling with. Even if she had tried to act tough the day before in the boathouse, he'd seen through it. And more than that, more importantly perhaps, he wanted more with her.

Somewhere around four in the morning when he'd finally given up on any chance of real sleep, the solution to his problem had come to him. He was trying way too hard to keep her at arms' length when all he really wanted to do was wrap her up in his arms and kiss her until she dropped all her defenses. He'd heard his father's voice in his head telling him to stay away from relationships long enough. It was time to listen to his heart. Just because it hadn't worked out between him and Britt, years ago, didn't mean his father was right. He'd been a kid. And Britt wasn't Samantha. Not by a long shot. This was different. He knew it in his gut.

Once he'd made the decision, his mind settled and sleep came to him. Now all he had to do was make it through the day. He slid a pile of papers across the desk. But first, before any work, he had one more call to make.

He dialed the number he'd memorized and wasn't surprised when it wasn't Samantha who answered the phone, but her cook, Archer. His first impression of the man had been a good one, made even better after eating the burger he cooked. And Trent knew that his message to Samantha would be in good hands.

"Tell her that I'm looking forward to seeing her tonight."

"That's all you got?" Skepticism laced Archer's voice. "I know Sam, and you're going to have to do better than that."

Trent thought about it for a second. Archer was right. He was going to have to do a lot better. "Tell her that I think I'd be willing to let her be the captain if she's willing to go sailing and to meet me at nine."

"Okay." Archer drew out the word. "I'm going to assume she's going to have some idea of what this means?"

Trent couldn't keep the grin off his face. "She'll know."

"Alright, man. Good luck."

His plan in place, Trent hung up the phone and was finally able to settle into work. By filling the time with taking care of all the last-minute details on his list, the afternoon flew by and he was just about to close down his computer and find Dylan to head over to the festival when his brother found him.

"Trent." His office door flew open and his brother, looking rather disheveled, stood in the doorway. "I need your help. Now."

He hurried around his desk. "What's wrong? You look like hell."

"That's because I've been cleaning out fountains and filters for the last hour. We need your help. There's no way we're ever going to get it all done. Come on."

"Slow down." Trent followed his brother from the office and into the main corridor. "What are you—"

The question died on his lips as he saw the chaos in front of him. The normally serene space had been torn apart with what looked like pieces of pumps or mechanical debris piled on tarps. "What the hell?"

"This," Dylan waved his hand, "is what I'm talking about. Kurt finally figured out what was causing the fountains to stop working. It turns out that the minerals in the natural spring water we were running through the system basically overloaded the main pumps. Maintenance didn't account for the mineral-dense water and…" He waved his hand around again.

"Shit. Really?"

"Really."

"So how do we fix it? Can we—"

"The main pumps have been repaired and Kurt worked some sort of magic, basically treating the water that will go through the fountain system so it's not quite so problematic. The water in the pools will stay full strength springs water, but the decorative water has to be, pardon the phrase, watered down."

Relief coursed through him. Thank goodness his brother was on the job. "That's a relief." He looked at Dylan, who did not look as relaxed as he should considering the crisis had been averted. "What?"

"Don't get too comfortable yet. The main system is fixed,

but the water has left deposits in all the fixtures and they're not going to work until they're cleaned. Which means—"

"They won't be running for the opening."

"That's right." Dylan bent down and grabbed a wire brush from a nearby tool bag. "And given the sheer number of water features you insisted on at the resort, it's all hands on deck, brother." He slapped the brush into Trent's hand. "We have a lot of work to do to get everything up and running."

EVERYTHING WAS IN PLACE. As Samantha walked through the room, she marveled at how it could even be her Grizzly Paw. The place was entirely transformed. Jules had done an amazing job. How an eleven-year-old could pull off such a feat was beyond her, but she was more than impressed. And it hadn't mattered to the girl that the majority of the festival took place outside; she insisted that the Grizzly Paw look the part as well. It was stunning.

Paper pom poms in bright summery colors hung from every available ceiling space to give the room an almost surreal feeling as the lights illuminated the tissue and cast a multicolored glow throughout the space.

Even though Trent had said the budget wasn't an issue, Sam still encouraged Jules to do it on the cheap, so she'd dug around in the storeroom and found a box of unused mason jars that she'd filled with wildflowers and placed on all the tables and along the front bar. The whole space looked, well, summery—which was the point. As Sam moved through the room, enjoying the way her skirt of the red sundress she'd picked out just for the occasion floated around her bare legs, she let her hand trail along the tables and chair backs and a feeling of what could only be described as happiness washed over her.

It was fleeting, however, as thoughts of Trent intruded on her good mood. Given the day before, she should have been feeling good. Better than good—she should have been floating through the day. But during the night, of which she'd slept very little, she'd come to a realization. Despite her best efforts, she'd fallen in love with Trent.

If pressed, she couldn't have explained it to anyone but there was no other way to account for the tingle in her belly whenever she thought of him, the heat that washed over her making it almost impossible to function, and the overall ache in her heart when she realized her feelings were definitely not reciprocated. Trent wasn't a relationship kind of guy. He was all business. And even on the off chance that he did want more than one night with her, she'd done her best to make sure he knew she wasn't interested.

"God." She spoke aloud to the empty room. "I've been such a bitch."

"It happens sometimes. But you look hot. You really should wear your hair down more often."

Sam turned around to see Beth, dressed in her gorgeous dress, her hair piled high on her head, standing at the bar. "Sorry," she said. "I know you're not open for the festival yet."

"For you, I'm always open."

Needing her best friend more than ever, Sam pulled her into a hug, careful not to crumple her dress.

"What was that?" Beth asked kindly. "Just needed a hug for some reason?"

Sam nodded.

"And I bet I could guess what that reason is." Sam didn't bother to protest. "Does the reason start with a T?"

Beth took Sam's hand and led her to a nearby table. "Talk."

Sam sighed. "I think I'm in love."

Beth couldn't have smiled any wider if she'd just been

proclaimed Miss Cedar Springs. She jumped up and down and clapped her hands like a schoolgirl. "That's so amazing," she squealed. "And Trent is perfect. Tall, dreamy, successful, and oh so yummy."

Sam narrowed her eyes and tipped her head. "I don't think you should be thinking about your boss like that."

"He's not my direct boss. Besides, it's the truth."

Sam didn't bother to answer; instead, she devoted her attention to a napkin that she suddenly felt needed to be ripped into tiny pieces.

"Wait." Beth slapped her hand down on the table. "If you're in love, shouldn't you be happy? Lord knows I'm no expert, but from my very limited experience I think you should be dancing and shouting it out and at the very least, smiling."

Sam looked at her best friend. She was glad she was back in Cedar Springs, and hadn't Trent made that happen? Even if it was indirectly. For that, she'd always be grateful to him. And even if it wasn't possible to be with him, she couldn't stand around and mope about it. "It's fine," she said after a minute. "I think I just got my hopes up for something that wasn't there."

"How do you know?"

"Pardon?"

"You're a smart woman, Sam. Strong, too."

Sam waited. "And?"

"And…I've never known you to be such a wimp."

Sam's mouth dropped open.

"Seriously," Beth continued, obviously on a roll. "The Sam I know goes after what she wants and at the very least doesn't sit by and let it slip away without so much as a peep. Are you seriously going to let it go? Just like that? Without saying one word to him? That doesn't sound like the strong, independent, determined woman I know. Does it?"

"Well…I…there doesn't seem to be…oh for God's sake,

you're right." Sam pushed up from the table. "I'm being a total baby about it all."

Beth nodded in agreement. "You are."

"Thanks for that." She gave her friend a smirk. "But you're right. I at least have to say something. How else will I ever know what could have been?"

"Or what could be. Besides, maybe he feels the same way." Beth leaned back in her chair and crossed her bare legs.

For a moment, Sam allowed herself to consider that possibility. She remembered the way he'd looked into her eyes, the tender way he'd touched her and stroked her hair. "No." She shook her head, not letting herself get her hopes up. "But at least this way I'll know for sure. I'll say something when I see him later." She smoothed her hands down her dress and fluffed her hair—that she'd worn down on purpose—back, behind her shoulders. She took a deep breath and as she exhaled, let the stress and worry of the last twenty-four hours go with it. "Thank you. Sometimes I need a bit of Beth in my life."

"And that's why I'm here, darling." She blew Sam a kiss. "Now go and make this the best summer solstice festival the town of Cedar Springs has ever seen. How can it not be? We have Jacked Crackers, for goodness' sake. I read an article on them last month, and the guitar player, Slade, is kind of cute." She batted her eyelashes and Sam laughed.

"Slade?" She eyed her friend knowingly. "Don't tell me you go for the rock star type?"

Beth stood and joined her. "You know I don't. That would be the last type of guy I'd need or want in my life. But hey, a girl can dream, can't she?"

Chapter Ten

AS THE SUN SET, the party was in full swing and Sam's mood lifted just walking through the transformed field area that was full of her friends and neighbors all laughing, dancing, and having a great time. Jules had worked her magic on the outside area, too. With the help of her new friends, she'd strung an incredible amount of twinkling lights through the trees, and pulled some old patio lanterns across the dance floor, which was really just a few large sheets of plywood that Archer had arranged to be donated by the hardware store.

"How about a dance?"

Preston. With everything going on with Trent, she'd totally forgotten about him. "No time to dance." She shrugged. "I have a party to run."

"I think the party is running itself." Preston ran the back of his hand down Sam's bare arm, causing a chill to run through her. Suddenly the gentle breeze blowing off the lake was too much. She pulled away and wrapped her arms around her waist. "You look beautiful, Sammie. I can't remember the last time I saw your hair like that."

She touched her hair self-consciously, before remembering

why and who she'd worn it that way for. "Thanks, Preston. I feel good. But I'm also very busy tonight. I'm sure there's some single woman who'd be happy to dance with you."

"But it's not you?" He tipped his head in question and batted his eyelashes in the pouty way that for some bizarre reason used to work on her when they were younger.

"No." She laughed. "It's not me."

Even if she put herself out there and Trent rejected her, Sam knew in that moment as she looked at the man who'd occupied so much of her time that now that she'd had a taste of what real passion and love—even if it might be one-sided—looked like, she'd never go back to what she had with Preston. Never.

"No," she said again, this time with a big smile. "It's definitely not going to be me." Leaving him staring after her, she walked away, being sure to wiggle her hips so the skirt swished around her bare legs in a way that she knew was killer.

The band was onstage, finishing up their first set, and it didn't seem to matter to the older residents that they had no idea who the Jacked Crackers were; they were dancing right along with everyone else. She had to admit, the band was a success. It didn't seem to matter, Sam thought as she danced her way across the dance floor. No matter what was playing, the people of Cedar Springs were in a partying mood and the fact that she brought it to them made her glow with pride. She tried not to think of the expenses, even if they were smaller than she'd forecasted, what with Jules doing the decorations and Trent providing a band. A stack of bills on her desk would still need to be paid. She'd worry about it later.

Sam pushed her concerns from her mind and went to find Jacked Crackers backstage. She gave her name to their security team and the beefy bouncer let her past. Thank goodness they'd thought to bring their own security, because it hadn't even occurred to Sam that they might need some. The life of a rock star, or musician or whatever, was so far from her reality, she hadn't given it much thought beyond the music they'd be playing.

The backstage area wasn't much more than some tables and chairs arranged in a loose circle. There was a curtain that had been draped up around the space, presumably to give them privacy. And all in all, it was actually kind of cozy.

"That was great," she said to the guys as they came offstage. "The crowd loves you."

The men nodded and smiled as if they heard that all the time, which they probably did considering they were big news pretty much everywhere.

"It's cool playing a small town." A particularly scruffy, yet very good-looking man who Sam recognized as one of the guitar players, said. "We usually play big arenas, with the crowd screaming and—"

"It's awesome," one of his bandmates interrupted him. "Chicks screaming and throwing themselves at—"

"Shut up, man." The guitar player punched his friend and stood, putting distance between him and his bandmate. "Sorry about Cal. He's a drummer and…well, anyway I'm sorry you had to hear that." He ran his hand through his scruffy dark hair before offering it to Sam. "I'm Slade."

"Slade?"

He nodded and shrugged. It was easy to see why Beth thought he was so cute. But she was right, a rock star was definitely not the type of guy she needed in her and Jules's life. Especially after what she'd just overheard.

"Nice to meet you."

"I want to thank you for letting us play your gig." Slade's smile was genuine, and despite the fact that he was probably used to people fawning all over him, Sam could see there was a real guy under the facade.

Sam laughed. "No," she said. "I'm pretty sure I should be

the one thanking you. We really appreciate you guys coming out to play such a small town."

"It's a nice change. We usually play such big places that you can't connect with the audience, you know?"

Sam didn't know, but she nodded.

"And we're about to go on tour again," Slade continued.

There was a flash of something in his eyes when he spoke. Regret maybe? Sam didn't have time to think on it because the lead singer, Axel, who she'd been introduced to earlier, joined them. "Everything okay, boss?"

"I'm hardly the boss." She smiled, relaxing. "And yes. Everything's great. You guys sounded awesome. Everyone's having a great time. Do you guys have everything you need? Because if you need anything, I can get…Archer?" She stared as he walked into the circle and placed a tray full of appetizers and drinks on the table in front of the guys. "I guess you have everything you need."

"We're good, love. Arch has been taking good care of us all afternoon." Both men went immediately to the food and joined their bandmates in devouring the offering.

"Oh, I bet he has." She shot Archer a look, but he just smiled and shrugged.

"You were busy. Someone had to do it."

"Uh huh." She bit her lip to keep from smiling. "I didn't take you for the groupie type."

Her friend's face flashed with shock and then a very rare blush before he smiled and said, "Little-known fact, but I've always wanted to be in a band."

Sam narrowed her eyes. "But you don't play an instrument."

"Details."

"And we'd love to have him, too," Axel called. He held up a chicken wing. "With food like this, you can be our road manager." The other guys grunted in agreement as they devoured the food in front of them.

"No deal." Sam laughed. "He's mine and you can't have him." She grabbed his arm and led him away to a quiet corner. "Is everything good to go back here?"

"I got it covered, Sammie. Nothing for you to worry about. I promise."

She nodded. "Thank you. So they'll go back on, sing for a bit—"

"A set," Archer corrected. "They'll play a set."

"Okay, fine. They'll play a set." She looked to him for approval and when he nodded, she continued. "And then the toast to the summer around ten. And then they'll si—I mean, play another set."

Archer laughed. "You'll get it."

"Uh huh." She smoothed her dress again. She still hadn't seen Trent, and she was beginning to get nervous that he wouldn't come. "Hey," she asked, changing tack. "You haven't seen Trent, have you? Has he come to check on…what?"

Archer's face underwent a transformation that made her breath catch.

"Oh shit."

"What?"

"I totally forgot." He dug through his back pocket and produced a crumpled napkin. "I'm such an ass." He thrust the napkin at her. "Here."

It wasn't like Archer to forget anything, and it really wasn't like him to look so stricken. She opened the napkin slowly, smoothing it out before she could decipher Archer's scrawl. She stared at the words for a moment, and read them once. And then again, before looking up at him.

"Sam," he started before she could say anything. "I'm sorry. It totally slipped my—"

"What time is it?"

"Sammie, don't be mad. I really am sorry. I can't—"

"What time is it?"

Archer blinked and pulled his cell phone out of his back pocket. "Almost nine thirty."

"What?" Sam took a deep breath and forced herself to calm down. It was only half an hour after when he said he'd be there. It wasn't the end of the world, or more accurately, the end of her chance with Trent.

"I'm sure you can still—"

"I got it." She smiled, more to calm herself than to placate Archer. "I just need you to take care of…" She waved in the band's general direction. "They should go on soon."

"I got it." He waved her away. "Go take care of whatever it is you need to take care of with Trent." He winked at her. "And I do hope it's what I think it is."

Sam stopped in mid-turn and stared at him. "And what is it that you're thinking?"

"I'm thinking the two of you need to get over yourselves and make it happen already. This is ridiculous." He grinned. "Am I wrong?"

"No." She laughed. "You're not wrong."

INSTEAD OF GOING BACK through the crowd, Sam dodged along the outside of the clearing, weaving through the trees and skirting along the shoreline. With the sun starting to set over the lake, the reflection of the mountains was cast in a beautiful combination of oranges, pinks, and purples. It was one of her favorite times of the day, and with everyone in town at the festival, it was perfectly calm and quiet on the water. Normally she would have stopped and enjoyed every second until the sun dipped low behind the mountain peaks.

But it wasn't a normal situation. From the moment she'd

decided to tell Trent how she felt about him, she'd been on edge, but knowing he wanted to see her too...knowing he might feel the same way...it was too much. Maybe she'd finally get that summer solstice kiss and she'd get her happy ever after.

She laughed out loud and picked her way across the pebbly beach when a noise stopped her.

A shadowy figure, maybe a girl, was sitting by the water's edge, her knees up and her head on her lap. Something was familiar about the figure.

"Jules?"

The girl turned her head and sniffed loudly, wiping her arm across her face.

Dammit.

Sam glanced down the beach in the direction of the boathouse and back at Jules. No contest. She slid her shoes off and let them dangle from her finger. It was easier to walk in sand and pebbles without the heels, even if they weren't very high.

"Hey." She put her hand on the girl's shoulder and squeezed. "What are you doing down here? I don't know if you heard, but there's a party going on up there."

Jules nodded and wiped at her face. She attempted a smile, but even in the dim light, Sam could see there was no effort behind it.

She dropped her shoes, and fluffed out her skirt, kneeling on the rough beach next to the girl she loved as her own. "What's going on, Jules? Talk to me."

"It's just...I don't..."

"Yes..."

"I don't have anyone to kiss tonight," Jules blurted.

The confession was so sudden and unexpected, Sam almost toppled backwards in the sand. "Wait," she said after a moment. "What?"

"I don't have anyone to kiss and isn't it a legend that

whoever you kiss at the summer solstice festival will be your love for the season?"

Sam shrugged. She couldn't deny it. The legend had been in existence as long as she could remember. And only seconds before, she'd been wishing like a silly schoolgirl herself for her own kiss. Not that she was going to share that particular piece of information with Jules at that moment.

"I'm not going to tell you it's a silly legend." The girl looked at her, her mouth agape. Certainly she expected Sam, a reasonable adult, to tell her the whole thing was ridiculous. "When I was your age, I believed it, too. But you know what? I've never kissed anyone at the summer solstice."

"Never?"

Sam shook her head. "Never."

"Is that why you aren't married?"

Sam laughed. Leave it to a kid to simplify things. "It's possible. But my point is, that kiss doesn't have to happen at twelve or twenty, or…any time really. Not before you're ready. The person you're meant to love, whether it's for a season or for a lifetime, will show up when you're ready." As she spoke, her own words resonated in her head. "And there's no reason to panic or make a big deal about it until then. In fact," she stood and took Jules's hand, hauling her up as well, "the best thing to do while you're waiting for that moment is to live your life and have fun. And that's exactly what you should be doing."

Jules nodded. "Maybe you're right."

"Oh, I know I'm right." Sam dusted off her dress. "You're only eleven. You have lots of time for kisses. Now go and have some fun."

She smiled and gave Sam a quick, hard hug. "Thank you." She turned to skip away, back to the party but turned around before she left and asked, "Are you coming?"

"Not yet. I have something to do. But I'll be there soon."

"Make sure you're in time for the toast to summer," Jules called. "Even if you have no one to kiss."

"Don't worry. I can't miss the toast," she said almost ruefully. "I do the toast."

Sam smiled after the girl. She really was a good kid and she'd be alright. What girl wasn't full of angst and worry at that age? Hell, she still was. She almost laughed at herself as she picked up her shoes and hurried across the beach to the boathouse. It was way after nine by that point. And maybe Trent had decided not to wait. Or worse, what if he'd waited for her and when she hadn't shown up, he'd decided she wasn't interested? After all, the last time she'd seen him, she hadn't really given him any reason to think she was.

Sam picked up the pace and as she reached the small house, she held her breath. Slowly, she walked around to the front. Nothing. "Trent?" Her voice was little more than a whisper, and the pit in the bottom of her stomach grew heavy with what she knew to be true. He wasn't there.

Still, she moved around the outside of the boathouse, holding out the slightest hope he was just around the corner. And after she'd circled it twice and the realization hit, she let herself feel disappointed, but only for a minute. What had she just told Jules? If it wasn't meant to be, it wasn't. And no matter how she felt about Trent, if he wasn't willing to wait for her, then it wasn't right. Because dammit if she was going to let herself be a victim of some stupid mix-up. It was all way too old-school for her.

Despite the mental pep talk she gave herself, Sam couldn't shut off the voice in her head that kept protesting that she actually did care.

THE FOUNTAINS WERE FIXED. Water was flowing through them and everything was set for opening day. That was the good news. The bad news was it was after eight when Trent finally finished up at the hotel, and drove as fast as he could, hoping his new buddy Officer Anderson was at the festival already and not lying in wait to give him another warning about speeding on the mountain roads.

He hadn't bothered to change his clothes that were covered in grime. Even if he was trying to make a good impression and finally tell Samantha that he'd fallen completely in love with her, he'd have to do it in dirty clothes. It wouldn't matter, though, if she thought he'd stood her up. Repeated calls to the pub had gone unanswered, not that he was surprised. The festival would be in full swing by now and he hadn't really expected anyone to answer the phone, although it would have been nice.

Trent managed to find a parking spot down the street from the pub. The minute he got out of his car, the music of the Jacked Crackers hit him. They sounded great, as they always did, and he smiled as he jogged toward the sound. He skipped past the bar and headed for the field and the crush of people milling about. Everyone was singing, laughing, and dancing. By all accounts, it looked like the festival was a roaring success. But as far as Trent was concerned, the night would not be declared successful until he had Samantha in his arms again.

He didn't bother going through the crowd, but ducked around the outside of the clearing, cutting through the trees until the boathouse came into view. What were the odds she'd waited for him for an entire hour? Especially on such a busy and important night. And that was assuming she'd come at all. What if Samantha got his message and disregarded it? The thought slammed into him. Of course it was a possibility. But it was one he'd done his best to ignore. He jogged the rest of the way, but no one was there.

She hadn't come.

He'd been wrong?

No. He knew in his heart she felt the same way. It was in the way her body responded to him, the way she'd looked up at him, her eyes so open, so full of…

"Samantha."

A flash of movement caught his eyes. It was her. It had to be her. The dark night made it hard to be sure, but he caught a glimpse of a woman moving away from him, in the opposite direction he'd come.

"Samantha," he called again as the figure stepped into the light of the party.

It was her. But she hadn't heard him call after her.

He swore under his breath and jogged back toward the crowded party, determined not to let her get away, because she'd been there. Waiting. His heart soared with an unfamiliar flutter.

By the time he reached the edge of the party and stepped through the trees into the lit clearing, she'd disappeared again. He scanned the crowd, desperately searching for her among the mostly unfamiliar faces. There was one face that looked familiar, and he pushed his way through the throng of people to talk to Jules.

"Hey, squirt."

She glared up at him and made a somewhat discreet gesture with her head to the group of kids she was standing with.

"Sorry," he mouthed to her. "The place looks amazing. You did a great job."

"Thanks." The girl beamed with pride and Trent noted she looked a lot more confident than in the past few days, too. Happier even. Good. She deserved it.

"Have you seen Samantha?" He didn't even try to sound cool and calm. "I need to talk to her about something."

Jules pointed to the stage, where Jacked Crackers had just quit playing. There she was. Looking incredible and feminine in a red dress that hugged all of her beautiful curves, Samantha stepped out onto the stage. She smiled at the band, flipping her hair back behind her shoulder in a flirty way that made him unreasonably jealous.

"What's she doing?" He didn't realize he'd asked the question until Jules answered.

"It's time for the toast to summer," she said. "It's the best part of the festival because after the toast is when the lanterns are released."

"Lanterns?"

On stage, Samantha started speaking, thanking the band for playing and everyone for coming to the festival. Trent listened with one ear, while he tried to figure out what Jules was talking about.

"Yup." She had a dreamy look on her face while she spoke. "And when the lanterns are all floating in the air, that's when you can make your sweetheart yours." Jules shook her head to clear her expression. "At least according to legend, that's what's supposed to happen." She shrugged, trying to appear nonchalant.

"Wait." Trent focused on the girl. "How do you make your sweetheart yours?"

She shrugged and rolled her eyes as if he was missing the entire point of the conversation. "You kiss her, of course. The legend goes that whoever you kiss at the summer solstice festival will be yours for the season."

"Is that right?" He turned back to the stage, a smile wide across his face. "Well, that sounds like a very good legend indeed."

SAM HATED SPEAKING in front of large groups, but everyone who was watching her and listening to her every word was family. The town of Cedar Springs, and everyone in it, was her family and she'd do anything to protect them. Even though she realized now that the Springs and Trent Harrison were not the enemy. In fact, the resort could save the town. She saw that now.

She squeezed the microphone tight and spoke again, addressing the crowd. "This year marks a big change for our little town," she said. "The Springs resort is set to open tomorrow and…" She paused, listening to some random cheers, a few boos, but mostly silence as the townspeople waited to see how she'd react. She took a breath. Even if things weren't meant to be with Trent, the Springs was meant for the town of Cedar Springs. It was a good match. Sam exhaled and said, "I want to be the first to officially welcome the Harrison brothers and the Springs resort to town. You've provided jobs and opportunities for this town and the people I love most." She caught Beth's eye and smiled. "And for that we should all be thankful." There were a few cheers and a smattering of applause, so Sam added, "Also, our wonderful band, Jacked Crackers, was brought to us by the Springs." With that, the crowd broke out in a roar and Sam knew it would be okay. There would still be a few holdouts who objected to the tourists, but sometimes change was good and the people of Cedar Springs would see that.

The band played a quick chorus of their hit song, which amped up the crowd even more, winning everyone over to their side. Sam took the opportunity to signal to Kylie to hand out the remaining lanterns. She grabbed her own from Archer, who joined her onstage and waited until the roar of the people calmed down.

"It's time for the toast to summer." She tried to keep her voice from shaking. She'd been so sure she'd be standing in front of everyone with Trent, ready to finally have her chance at making the legend come true. "Please raise a glass in honor of the sun and may your days be hot…"

"And your nights be hotter," the crowd chanted in unison in the traditional toast.

Sam laughed, and took a sip of the cocktail Archer had handed her. His eyes were full of questions, no doubt wanting to know how things went with Trent. She looked away to keep her heart from breaking, and took the lantern from him instead.

"Sam?" He whispered her name in question, but she simply shook her head. She couldn't talk about it. Not now.

She waited a moment for everyone to get their lanterns lit. It was her favorite part. When the night sky filled with the paper lanterns, the entire effect was nothing short of magical. No wonder it had become the perfect time for true love to bloom.

"Sam?" Archer whispered her name again, but she ignored him. Biting her lip to keep from crying, she spoke into the microphone. "On the count of three, release your lantern and let summer begin." She took a deep breath, and scanned the crowd, taking in her friends and fellow townspeople standing with their sweethearts, ready to seal the onset of summer with a kiss.

"One." Her eyes landed on Jules. She stood with a group of kids; none of them looked as if they'd be doing any kissing. She winked at her, and Jules smiled.

"Two." Preston was standing in the middle of the dance floor, chatting up a young woman Sam didn't recognize. She tried not to laugh. Looked like he'd get his kiss after all. She shook her head and kept looking through the crowd but when she couldn't see what her body and heart so desperately wanted to see, Sam knew she couldn't put it off any longer.

She licked her lips, and swallowed hard, raising the microphone to her mouth.

"Three."

But it wasn't her that spoke the word. As the crowd released their lanterns into the air with a cheer, she turned to see the man who'd given the final signal.

"Trent."

He stood so close to her, her senses filled with his familiar scent. Her body shook slightly; a chill, not caused by the night air, ran through her as he reached out, gently caressing her cheek with his touch.

"From what I understand, we're supposed to let this go together." His hand rested on hers that still held the lit lantern.

Sam looked into his eyes, unable to speak as she released her grip on the lantern. Together, they looked up and followed its path into the sea of paper lights set against the stars that were starting to appear. When she lost track of which lantern was theirs, she looked away but the tears in her eyes blurred his features.

His thumb smoothed away a stray tear that streaked down her cheek. His other arm wrapped around her waist and pulled her against his hard chest. When his mouth lowered to hers, she returned his kiss with all the pent-up feelings and emotions she'd been holding inside. Unaware or uncaring of who was watching them, there was no need for words.

Finally, Sam pulled away and bit her lip. "You know what this means?"

Trent's smile reached his eyes. "According to legend, it means that you're my sweetheart for the season."

Sam nodded, unable to hide the happiness flowing through her.

"But I don't believe in legends." His voice turned serious, and Sam's heart paused for a moment. "Because a season isn't good enough."

"What?"

"I love you, Samantha Burke. And a season just isn't going to be long enough for me to show you just how much you've gotten under my skin and into my heart."

She reached up and let her fingers slide through his hair. "I've never been a big believer in legends myself."

"So, you…"

"I love you, too." Her lips curled up into a smile. "Despite my best efforts to keep you out, you've somehow managed to push your way into my heart. And I wouldn't have it any other way."

Trent laughed, and a whoop went up from the crowd when they once more sealed their declarations with a kiss. It wasn't until the band started playing that they reluctantly broke apart.

Axel, the lead singer, sidled up them. "Glad you found your man, love. I'm happy to give you the stage, but these folks are looking for a show."

Sam laughed. "Point taken." She led Trent offstage, and out of the spotlight. But not ready to let go yet, she said, "About that message you left…"

He tilted his head and eyed her. "What about it?"

"Are you still looking to go for a sail?"

It was Trent's turn to laugh, but there was nothing but lust in his eyes when he looked at her. "Aye aye, Captain."

Epilogue

WITH THE SUN high in the sky, the weather was perfect for a Sunday afternoon. Made even more perfect by the fact that Sam had closed the Grizzly Paw, like she did every Sunday, and was enjoying the beautiful weather on the back deck surrounded by friends, catching up on the week.

"Come on," Trent said to her. "You can admit it now. It's been two months, and the Springs has been good for business. Hasn't it?"

Sam wrinkled her nose at him and refilled Carmen and Dylan's glasses from the jug on the table instead of answering him.

"He's right," Archer chimed in. "And you know I hate admitting that."

Trent nodded and his grin widened.

"Okay, okay." Sam gave in. "You were right. The resort has been good. We've been busier than ever and although I still have some catching up to do, things actually look good."

"I'll drink to that." Dylan raised his glass.

The circle of friends all toasted to the success of the Springs, to their town and to friends, new and old.

"So," Beth said with a sly smile in Sam's direction. "I heard a rumor."

"Oh yeah?" Carmen leaned forward.

"Yup." Beth turned and pinned Sam with her gaze. "I heard there's a certain hotel suite that's empty most nights."

Both Sam and Trent blushed, but it was Trent who finally said, "I'm trying to convince our girl here to move up to the resort with me."

"No way," Sam cut in. "I need to be here at the bar. Trent's moving down here."

"Is he?" Dylan tilted his head and gave his brother a wry grin.

"No."

"Yes."

They both spoke at the same time before locking eyes in a stare down that held more heat than was probably appropriate around friends.

"Looks like I started something." Beth laughed and raised her glass to her lips before putting it down and calling out, "Rhys. You're here."

EVERYONE TURNED to look in the direction of Rhys Anderson, the local sheriff, and good friend, who was making his way around the back of the building to the deck.

"Hey buddy." Archer pulled up a chair for him, and Rhys dropped his large frame in it.

For Rhys, it had been a long week. And it wasn't over yet. He still had at least another hour left before he could relax for the evening and have a beer with his friends. A much anticipated beer. As it was, he'd have to settle for some good company and maybe if he was lucky, some of Archer's nachos.

"Good to see you guys," he said, and meant it. With the afternoon sun shining down on you while you gazed out over the lake and caught up with your buddies, there was nowhere better to be.

Trent, Sam, Carmen and Dylan, his two newest friends, greeted him with a wave and a smile. Beth gave him a chaste kiss on the cheek when he sat down next to her. There was a time when he thought he'd end up marrying Beth, but things changed as they tended to do when you were kids, and now they were just good friends. He watched her from the corner of his eye. At least that's what he kept telling himself. Maybe there was still a chance for them?

He didn't have time to dwell on the thought, because before he knew it, he was swept up in the conversation and a beer was placed in front of him.

"Not for me." He pushed it away. "I still have an hour on my shift."

"And you think you're going to get a call in the next hour?" Dylan asked. "In this sleepy little town?"

"Sleepy?" Rhys scoffed. "Maybe once it was. But ever since you boys showed up…"

Trent gave him a friendly punch on the arm. "You love it," he said. "It gives you something to do."

Rhys nodded and accepted the iced tea Sam handed him instead. "I do." He held up his drink to toast before taking a large gulp.

"I think what you really love is handing out speeding tickets to innocent drivers." Trent peered over his sunglasses at him.

"Only you, buddy," Rhys fired back at Trent. "And maybe not so innocent." In the eight weeks since they'd met and the resort had officially opened, Trent had managed to score two speeding violations and an impressive four warnings. "If you're not careful, you're going to set some sort of record."

Sam shot her boyfriend a look and turned back to Rhys. "Want something to eat?"

"I'd love something. But you don't have to—"

But she was already up from the table. "For Cedar Springs finest?" She gave him a knowing smile. Rhys wasn't about to turn his nose up to food. Especially since he'd barely had enough time to stop at the grocery store, let alone cook anything for himself. If he had any culinary skills at all. Which he didn't.

"Thanks, Sam." He smiled. "I'd really appreciate it."

She waved away his thanks. "I'll be right back."

"And get Archer out here," Beth called after her.

The group lapsed into easy conversation and when Archer and Sam rejoined them, the talk turned to the resort and how busy everyone was keeping things at the Springs running smoothly. All except Sam, who had her hands full with her pub and the increased business she'd experienced, too.

"I have to admit," Sam said. "And you know I won't say this again." She narrowed her eyes at Trent before continuing. "You were right. The resort was good for business."

"I knew it." He jumped to his feet and did a ridiculous fist pump. "She never admits when she's wrong."

"I didn't say I was wrong." Sam held up a finger. "Just that you were right. There is a distinct difference."

"Uh huh." Beth rolled her eyes and they all laughed.

"Well, I'm glad the Grizzly Paw is doing so well," Carmen declared. "Because there is no better place in town to come and enjoy the summer sun."

"Not even the—"

"Not even the pools at the Springs," Carmen interrupted Dylan. "I love it there, but there's nothing like the lake in the summer."

"And good friends," Dylan added.

"Too bad summer's almost over and I've barely had time to enjoy it," Rhys mused.

Carmen groaned. "No. Don't rush it. It may be the end of August, but surely it'll stay hot for a bit, won't it?"

Sam shrugged. "It's hard to tell in the mountains. If we're lucky, it might stay nice."

"Well, we better get lucky," Carmen said and Dylan wiggled his eyebrows.

Rhys laughed along with the others. "I'm with you, Carmen. I need a—"

"Officer Anderson?" His radio crackled with the familiar voice of Janice, the police dispatcher. He tried to stifle his sigh while everyone at the table groaned their sympathy.

"I'm here, Janice. What's up?"

"There's been an…"

"Come in?" Rhys hit the button on his radio. "I didn't copy, Janice."

"Granite and Pine." The voice crackled.

He'd heard enough. It was only a few blocks away. Heck, everything in Cedar Springs was only a few blocks away. He shoved up from the table. "Gotta go," he said to his friends.

"I hope it's not serious." Concern shone in Beth's eyes, and for a minute, the old idea that maybe she had feelings for him flashed through his head. He shook it away. Even if by some miracle she did care about him after all these years of him pining for her, he could honestly say he didn't feel the same way anymore. Did he?

No. He'd moved on years ago. She might always have the power to make his head turn, but his heart was his own again.

"I'm sure it'll be fine," he said to Beth. "There may be a lot more people in town all of a sudden, but we don't have big city drama yet."

"We'll be waiting, buddy," Archer called. "I promise to save you a beer."

He waved in their direction and hopped down off the deck, speaking into his radio at the same time. "On my way, Janice."

He'd told his friends that there was no big city crime in Cedar Springs...and there wasn't, yet. It was just a matter of time. Although he had a pretty good guess that he was only heading into a minor situation, his heart still picked up the pace and he could feel the excitement starting to build. Despite trying to get clarification from Janice over the radio, nothing but static had come back. He had to see about getting those radios fixed. He liked to know what was going on, never mind the fact that it was a security issue. Even in a town the size of Cedar Springs...you never knew.

It only took a few minutes to make the quick drive to the corner of Granite and Pine, and just another second to spot the stalled car. He didn't recognize the woman in the front seat.

Rhys knew almost everyone.

Still, he didn't bother putting on the sirens or lights. It was only a stalled car after all.

But still, his cop instincts kicked into high gear as he pulled up behind the stalled car with its hood up and flashers on. Something wasn't right. Once more he tried the radio to call Janice—still nothing.

With a shake of his head, Rhys got out of his cruiser. *Nothing of note has ever happened in Cedar Springs,*

But still, he kept his hand on his weapon.

Who is in the car? And why is she in Cedar Springs? Find out what Kari, the beautiful new stranger in town is hiding, and if Rhys can break down her walls long enough to find out, in Falling Into Forever.

You can read a special excerpt of Falling Into Forever right after this—>

And if you want even more romance...click HERE for an exclusive FREE novella that isn't available anywhere else!

Falling into Forever

Please enjoy this special excerpt from Falling into Forever

The last thing Officer Rhys Anderson wanted to be doing on a sunny Sunday afternoon in Cedar Springs was responding to a random call out. Particularly considering he was almost finished with what had been a very long workweek.

"It couldn't have waited fifteen minutes," he muttered to himself as he guided his patrol car down the street after leaving his friends enjoying themselves at the Grizzly Paw pub. "Then Jones would have had to take care of it. Fifteen minutes." Rhys shook his head as he pulled up behind the stalled car, it's hood up and flashers on. The radios were on the fritz—again—so his dispatcher, Janice, hadn't been able to tell him what the call out was for. Which is why Rhys had one hand on his weapon as he made his way to the car.

"Hello?"

A flash of movement from the front of the car caught his attention and as a reflex, he pulled his gun and almost immediately cursed himself for doing so. He wasn't in the city anymore. It was goddamm Cedar Springs. Population, not enough for trouble. Just the way he liked it.

"Oh." A female voice squeaked. "I...I..."

Rhys lowered his weapon and holstered it at the sight of the petite woman he'd surprised. "I'm sorry, ma'am." He held his hand up and approached slowly. "I didn't mean to startle you. Is everything okay here?"

She stared at him for a moment. Her eyes darted down to his gun before she shook her head. "No," she said. "I mean, yes. They're fine."

Her voice shook and Rhys again cursed himself for being paranoid for pulling his weapon on a stalled car. He must be exhausted, and he was letting it get to him. There was no need for the big city dramatics. Especially now that he saw the unfamiliar woman, who was likely one of the many new tourists who had descended on the quiet town once the Springs resort opened up the hill. She was also remarkably beautiful. A fact that was definitely not lost on Rhys.

"Which is it?" He tried to keep his voice light. "Everything okay? Or not?"

She shook her head and opened her mouth to say something before she changed her mind. "No," she said. "Everything is not okay." She turned to face the engine again, and instead of following her gaze, Rhys studied her profile. Smooth, creamy skin, delicate features, and...a bruise.

"Ma'am." Rhys took a step forward and glanced down at the bumper of the car. "Are you hurt?"

"What?" She stared at him. "No. My car won't start."

"You didn't crash into anything?"

"What?" she asked again. "Why would you...Oh." Her hand flew to her head. Her fingers danced carefully over what looked to be a tender spot. "Yes." Her voice broke. "I had a bit of a fender bender the other day."

Rhys raised his eyebrow and looked again at the immaculate bumper of the sedan. Following his gaze, the woman added, "It was fixed up already. They were really quick."

He knew she was lying. His training had taught him to read the signs and body language, and her body language screamed that she was hiding something. But his training also taught him when to back off.

"Well, what seems to be the problem with the engine?" He put a smile on his face and moved under the hood. He didn't miss her soft exhale as he dropped the matter of the accident. "Maybe I can see what's going on."

"Thank you. I really am sorry to trouble you. I didn't mean for the police to come out but she insisted she should call."

"Wait." Rhys stepped back and turned his attention from the hoses and belts in front of him back to the beautiful woman whose name he still didn't know. "Who insisted?" As he asked the question, he knew the answer. He shook his head and ran a hand through his hair. "No. Let me guess. Sweet little old lady, about this tall." He held his hand somewhere around chest height. "Lives over there?" As Rhys pointed, they both turned and looked in the direction of the yellow house with the white porch. "Hi, Aunt Daisy," Rhys called. To the woman, he whispered, "She thinks I can fix anything."

"It's sweet."

He looked down into the most interesting eyes he'd ever seen. A blue so deep they were almost black; white flecks made them look almost like marbles he'd collected as a kid. Stunning. Especially since the owner of those eyes was smiling. The first he'd seen from her.

"I don't know about sweet." He waved at his aunt and turned back to the engine. He'd have to go over and say hi when he finished. It'd been too long since he'd been to visit. "Let's see if we can get this working for you...I'm sorry, you didn't tell me your name."

She flushed. Her skin turned a pretty shade of pink; the

blush spread down her neck, into her…Rhys lifted his eyes, forcing himself to focus on her face.

"It's Kar—Kari," she said. "Kari Fox."

"Okay." He nodded despite the fact that something seemed a bit off. "Kari."

It was a pretty name and it suited her. Delicate and feminine, but with an undercurrent of something more. Something he might like to investigate further.

She swallowed hard and bit her bottom lip. "Thank you, Officer. I probably—"

"Rhys," he cut her off. "Call me Rhys."

She nodded and clenched her hands together. "Can you fix it?"

"No."

Her face fell and for one terrible moment, Rhys was afraid she might cry.

"It looks like your timing belt is torn and honestly, the best thing to do is get it to Doug. He'll be able to tell you better than I can exactly what you're up against. But one thing is for sure. You're not going anywhere in this car for a few days."

Dammit. This couldn't be happening. She needed that stupid car. What good was a Mercedes if it wouldn't run when it was supposed to?

Her lip quivered and, afraid she would cry, Kari bit down on her lip again. She couldn't fall apart. Especially not in front of a cop. A very attractive cop. She pushed the thought from her head the moment it popped in. That was the last thing she needed.

"Kari," Rhys said. His voice was kind and concerned and for a moment, a very brief moment, Kari let her guard down. But then he reached for her.

Instinctively she jerked back, out of his reach. "No."

"Whoa." He held his hands up. "I'm sorry. I didn't mean to startle you. Again. Are you sure you're okay?"

She nodded and took a deep breath. She needed to calm down. This was ridiculous. He was just trying to help and she was acting like a freak. She needed to get a hold of herself. And quickly.

"I'm the one who should be sorry," she said. "You're just trying to help. I think I'm just tired. It's been a long day and I was really hoping to get farther today but this…" She waved her hand in the direction of the car and forced a smile. "What can you do? How do I get a hold of this Doug fellow?"

Rhys gave her a strange look. It hadn't been the first. She really needed to pull herself together or he would ask questions, and that would only lead to trouble.

"I'll call him for you and get your vehicle towed to the shop. Being Sunday afternoon, he's probably out fishing, but I'll see what I can do." He smiled and the dimple in his left cheek made an appearance. She'd noticed it the first time he'd smiled at her. It was so cute, and so totally at odds with the rest of his big, tough cop exterior. "Where are you staying?"

"Pardon?" She focused on what he was asking. "Staying?"

"Tonight? I'm going to guess you're up at the Springs?"

"The Springs?" she repeated, feeling more and more like an imbecile. "What's that?"

Rhys closed the hood of her car and wiped his hands on the legs of his uniform. "Grab your bags," he said. "I'll give you a lift up there."

She couldn't get in the car with him. She had to take control of the situation and figure out what she was going to do. Kari glanced around. They were in the middle of a residential street. There wasn't anyone around, except for the elderly lady from earlier, and Rhys— Officer Anderson, she mentally corrected herself. There was no point getting too friendly with him. He seemed nice enough and he was a police officer. That probably meant she could trust him, at least to take her to the hotel.

"Kari?"

His concerned voice broke through her racing thoughts. She forced what she hoped was a friendly smile. "Yes. Just let me grab my purse."

Slowly, she walked around to the side of the car and opened the passenger door. When she bent down to pick up her purse from the floor, she squeezed her eyes shut and used the moment to take a deep breath. Think, think.

When she straightened, she took a look through the window at Officer Anderson, who was speaking into his radio and not looking at her. Quickly, she opened the glove box, snatched the registration papers and stuffed them in her purse.

Kari grabbed her tote bag from the back seat and went around to meet the waiting officer.

"Ready?"

She nodded.

"Is that all you have? Just one little bag?"

Kari glanced down at her overnight bag. She'd grabbed what she could; it would have to do. "That's it."

"Well then, let's get going." His smile was bright, and there was that dimple again. Kari felt herself relax a little bit, but just a little bit as she slid into the front seat of the cruiser next to him. "Where were you headed, anyway?" He put the cruiser in gear and drove away with a wave at the woman who still watched from the porch.

The question caught her off guard, which was ridiculous because of course he was going to ask. And way out in the mountains the way she was, it wasn't as if there were a lot of excuses she could give him. Cedar Springs was hardly a "passing through" kind of town. She certainly couldn't tell him the truth. That the night before, after grabbing what she could, she'd gotten in the car and just drove as fast as she could away from the city, and her life. And she most certainly couldn't tell him that the car wasn't technically hers. Being a man of the law, he was sure to look at the situation a whole lot differently than she did.

"I'm...well..." Kari took a deep breath and forced a lightness she didn't feel into her voice. "Honestly. I wasn't headed anywhere in particular. I needed a break from work, so I thought I'd drive until I found a nice little town to get some R&R." It wasn't totally a lie.

"Really?"

She nodded.

"I've never heard of anyone actually doing that before." He shrugged. "But good for you. And, you definitely landed in the right town. It's beautiful in Cedar Springs at the end of summer. And it looks like we're going to have a nice fall."

She nodded politely and turned to look out the window. He was right. The town was beautiful. She'd never heard of it before, which wasn't totally surprising considering the only holidaying she'd really done was for Brice's business travels, and that certainly didn't include picturesque mountain towns.

But she didn't want to think about Brice. That was the whole idea of leaving. So she didn't have to think of him. Or see him.

"Where is it we're going?" she asked, when they turned out of the town and onto a much more remote road. She clenched the seat and worked to control her breathing.

Officer Anderson glanced at her, and then did a second take. "Don't worry," he said. "The Springs is just up the mountain a way, but it's not too far. It just opened, so I'm sure we can get you a room and if not, I know the owners." He winked at her and she tried hard to relax. There was nothing to worry about as long as she was sitting in the front seat of the police car. Brice had no idea where she was and once the car was fixed, she'd get moving again. A few days wouldn't make too much difference.

Kari forced a smile. "It sounds nice."

But it was more than nice. She saw the sign first. The name of the resort was carved into a large rock, a waterfall gently cascading down next to it. It was beautiful. It was also very understated and classy. The hair on the back of Kari's neck stood up. She recognized upscale; it was like radar. Her fears were confirmed as they rounded the corner of the mountain road and she caught the first glimpse of the elegant building.

It wasn't as large as she would expect, but as they drove up the drive, she could see the building had been carefully designed. Without even going inside, she could imagine the interior.

"Isn't it something?"

Kari turned to the officer. "What type of hotel did you say this was?"

Officer Anderson beamed with obvious pride. "It was built around the natural hot pools," he said. "They're known for their healing properties and the Harrison brothers created a world-class resort to allow people to benefit. It's pretty amazing. I think you'll really like it."

No doubt about it, Kari thought. She would love it. But there was no way she could afford it. If she used her credit cards, Brice would know right away where she was, and she wasn't going to let that happen. Not until she could figure out what to do about her husband. Ex-husband, she quickly corrected herself. Regardless, she needed to figure something out. And quickly.

Rhys pulled up to the front door and put the car in park. He would have liked the drive to last longer, so he could get Kari talking a bit more. She was a hard one to figure out. Going from tense to, well, not totally relaxed, but at least less tense. He twisted in his seat to look at her.

"What do you think?"

"Officer—"

"Rhys." He interrupted her. "Please, call me Rhys."

"Okay." She swallowed hard and her hand fluttered to her chest. "The thing is…um…I don't know if the Springs is really the right place for me to stay."

All his senses went on high alert. There was something going on with this woman. Before he could say anything, she continued. "What with the car repairs and everything. Maybe it would make more sense for me to stay in town, to be closer to things. And they're probably all booked up already. I'd hate for you to have to talk to your friends."

Her eyes darted around, and when the valet opened the door, Rhys thought she might scream. Reflexively, he put a hand on her knee to still her. She jerked away, as if she was set to run out, but seeing the valet blocking her way, sat back hard in the seat.

"Give us a minute," Rhys said to the valet attendant. He raised his eyebrow and quietly clicked the door closed. Kari sagged back against the door.

"Are you okay?"

"I'm fine." She wouldn't look at him, but Rhys spotted her shaking hands. "I'm just a little jumpy. It's been a long day."

"Right." He drew out the word. There was something about her. His training told him to dig and ask the right questions to figure out what was going on with her. But all he really wanted to do was put his arms around her and pull her close to protect her from whatever it was that had her ready to run.

"Is there anywhere else I could stay?" she asked in a shaky voice. "Somewhere less…"

She didn't have to finish her sentence. It was money. The

Springs screamed expensive. Maybe he'd been wrong about her financial situation. He should know better than to judge someone by the type of car they drove. Maybe it wasn't her car? The thought flashed through his head. He hadn't even checked her license or registration. Of course, why would he? It was a broken down vehicle; she hadn't done anything wrong or given him any reason to be suspicious. Except for pretty much everything she'd said to him since they'd met.

"I have just the place," he said before he overanalyzed the situation any further. "My friend Sam has a room over her pub, the Grizzly Paw. It's right in town, and I could probably convince her to give you a good deal. We've been friends forever. Sound good?"

She nodded and the tentative smile on her face made Rhys forget any of the suspicions he had. He might be a cop, but he was also a man and there was no doubt about it, Kari was very beautiful. And he was a sucker for a damsel in distress.

Rhys put the car in gear and headed back down the mountain.

"You can come in if you want." Rhys put the cruiser in park in front of the Grizzly Paw and unclipped his belt. Knowing his friends the way he did, they'd still be on the back deck enjoying the last of the summer day, but he wasn't going to expose this clearly fragile woman to that rowdy bunch. No, he'd go in the front door and try to get things figured out quickly.

In response, Kari opened the door, clutched her tote bag to her chest, and got out of the car.

He shook his head and joined her in the gravel parking lot. "There's nothing to be worried about." He led the way up to the porch. "Sam's really nice and I know it isn't much, but her rooms are clean and comfortable, and you'll be——"

"I'm not worried."

The steel in her voice stopped him. Rhys turned and for the first time took her in. She was petite, but by no means small. Despite her strange hot and cold behavior, she really couldn't accurately be described as frail. She stood with her shoulders back, a hardness in her eyes as if she was trying to convince herself that her terrible day was going to turn out fine. She held her lips in a firm line, as if she was determined not to give up any indication of how she was feeling. "I believe you," he said after a moment, and meant it. He pushed the door open and waited for Kari to walk into the dimly lit bar.

Sam closed the Grizzly Paw on Sundays, but just like everyone else in Cedar Springs, she didn't lock the door. Besides, Rhys knew she was on the back deck with the rest of the gang, just the way she always was on Sunday afternoons, and just where he'd be, too. As soon as he finished getting Kari settled. He stole a glance at the woman. Maybe she'd like to join them?

"It doesn't look open."

"It's not." Rhys led the way across the room. "But it's fine. Just wait here. I'll pop outside and grab Sam." He gestured to the spacious deck they could see through the windows on the far wall. The lake glistened in the background, and Rhys felt the familiar pull to jump in the water as soon as he got a chance.

He took one more quick look back at Kari before heading outside.

"Hey," Dylan greeted him. "You're back. What was the call? You got it sorted out already?"

"Not really." As much as he'd love to talk about the mysterious woman with his buddies, it wasn't the time, and with a glance toward Beth, who watched him carefully, he realized it also wasn't the place. "Can I talk to you for a second, Sam?"

"Me?" The dark-haired bar owner pointed to her chest and

pushed her chair back. "Of course. I'm going to be right back," she said to the group. "So don't even think about drinking my beer." She looked directly at her boyfriend, and owner of the Springs resort, Trent, when she spoke. He responded by giving her a friendly smack on her bottom and a wink.

"No promises."

The group's laughter followed them as Rhys led Sam to the corner of the deck before going back inside.

"What's up?"

"I have a bit of a situation." Rhys glanced toward the window. Although he couldn't see in, he knew Kari could see them. "Do you still have that empty room upstairs?"

Sam shrugged. "Actually, I do. I haven't rented it in a while. Why? What's up?"

"The call out I just had…well, she needs a room. And the Springs is kind of out of the question." Sam nodded knowingly, and he knew she would trust his judgment. "It would only be for a night or two."

"That's fine." Sam's smile was warm and she was totally accepting of his explanation, as he knew she would be.

"Great," he said. "I'll take you to meet Kari. Her car broke down and she should only need the room for a few days until her car's fixed." As he spoke the words, he couldn't help but hope it would take longer than a few days. Maybe he'd have a chance to get to know her a bit better if she stuck around.

"Of course." Sam interrupted his thoughts. "Is she inside?"

He nodded and went to make the introductions.

The room wasn't much, but at least it was clean and cheap, at least compared to what the resort up the hill was sure to cost. Kari knew expensive when she saw it, and there was no way she would have been able to afford even the most basic room at that fancy hotel. Especially with only eighty dollars in her purse. No, she thought as she wandered over to the window, the accommodation at the Grizzly Paw would be much more affordable.

That was, as long as she didn't have to stay longer than one night. At seventy-five dollars a night, which she was pretty sure was a special rate because Rhys Anderson had brought her in, she wouldn't be able to afford more than one nights' stay, and that didn't include food or the gas she'd need to get out of Cedar Springs. She didn't even want to think about what the repairs would cost.

She let out a deep sigh and opened the window to let the breeze in. The view was amazing. She looked out over the lake. A few ski boats pulled wakeboarders behind them, and the odd canoe and kayak floated by, but mostly the water was empty. It sparkled in the late afternoon sun and Kari felt the pull to stick her toes in to see if it was as refreshing as it looked. Surely it wouldn't hurt to get outside and take a walk?

But first there was something she needed to take care of. She dug her prepaid cell phone from the depth of her tote bag and powered it up. No one knew where she was and it would be better if she kept it that way, but because she didn't have any type of plan before she ran off, it also meant she didn't have any money. And by the way things were shaping up, she was going to need some. Without a lot of options left, she dialed the number she knew by heart and held her breath.

When the familiar voice on the other end answered, she exhaled.

"Mom?"

"Karina? Is that you? Where are you? Everyone's been worried sick."

She doubted that very much.

"I'm fine, Mom."

"Karina, where are you?" Her mother's voice turned soft, and for a minute Kari thought maybe her mom did care. Maybe, after all these years, she finally believed her about Brice's continual mental abuse and would finally stand behind her only daughter and support her decision to leave.

Kari sank onto the bed. "I'm in a—"

"Brice will come and get you just as soon as you let us know where you are."

Kari bit her lip. She should have known.

"I know the two of you can work this out, honey," her mother continued. "It's just a misunderstanding."

"We're divorced, Mom."

"Karina." She could almost hear her mother wagging her finger at her. "You love Brice."

"No." Kari sat on the bed, and tried to roll some tension out of her shoulders. But it was true. She'd loved him once. When they'd met, Brice was charismatic and charming. He wined and dined her, told her how beautiful and amazing she was. She'd fallen hard and fast, hardly believing the fairy tale she was in. But that's all it had been. It didn't take long for the shine to wear off.

"Well, you loved him once," her mother continued. "You can do it again. And a divorce is just a piece of paper; it can be torn up."

"No." Kari let her shoulders sag. "It can't." Nor did she want it to be. The very last thing she wanted was to be associated with Brice Callahan in any way.

"Well, you didn't have to run away the way you did." The familiar bite in her mother's voice returned. "It's not like you were in any kind of danger or anything."

Yes. She was. It didn't seem to matter how many times Kari told her mother about Brice's escalating threats, the way just the night before, he'd had his police officer buddy come around under the pretense of warning her about some local break-ins, when what he was really telling her was that she wouldn't be safe. It didn't take a genius to read between those lines. No. She wasn't safe. It was only a matter of time before Brice acted out on one of his threats. Isn't that why she'd run? His last voicemail had been different. Edgier. Her instinct said to run.

"You're always so dramatic." Her mom broke through her thoughts. "Brice has been nothing but good to you, honey. If you would just come home, you could work out whatever it is that's got you all upset this time and I'm sure before long, things will go back to normal."

"No. They won't."

Nor did she want them to.

"Why did you call, Karina?" Her mother's question startled her. "If you have no intention of coming home, then why did you bother?"

The words hit her in the chest. As much as she knew—had known for years—that her mom cared more about Brice, or more accurately, his money, than she did her own daughter, Kari still held out hope that underneath the woman's greed, a mother still cared about her only child. "I thought you might want to know I'm safe." Kari didn't bother mentioning that she was also hoping her mom might be able to help her out with her money problems. Even she could see there was no point.

Laughter floated up through the open window and reached Kari's ears. After Sam had shown her up to the room, she'd extended the invitation to join her and her friends on the back deck. With the phone still up to her ear, Kari made her way back to the window and looked down. There they were. A group of people, her age, people she'd probably be friends with in another life. A life that didn't include her past.

"Where are you? I hear laughter. Are you at a party, Karina? You know how Brice feels about—"

"I know how he feels." Her voice was tight and controlled.

"And I don't care." She pressed the button to disconnect the call before her mother could say one more word. She didn't want to hear it.

Kari tossed the phone behind her and continued to look out the window. Officer Anderson—Rhys—was sitting among the group. He'd changed from his uniform, but Kari recognized the dark hair, the strong shoulders and the overall presence of the man. He had that commanding presence that so many men in uniform seemed to innately have. Was it the uniform? Or the man? She didn't know. Brice's officer friend, Roger, had that, too.

Only, when Roger had come to her newly rented condo to warn her, or more like threaten her, his presence had been suffocating. As if he sucked all the oxygen from the air simply by being in the room, he hadn't made her feel protected...safe. Not like Rhys did. In the short time they'd spent together, Kari felt as long as he was next to her, everything would be okay. And no matter how hard she tried, she couldn't remember the last time she'd felt that way.

Will Kari's secrets destroy everything, including a new relationship with Rhys?
Find out in Falling Into Forever!

About the Author

Elena Aitken is a USA Today Bestselling Author of more than forty romance and women's fiction novels. The mother of 'grown up' twins, Elena now lives with her very own mountain man in the heart of the very mountains she writes about. She can often be found with her toes in the lake and a glass of wine in her hand, dreaming up her next book and working on her own happily ever after.

To learn more about Elena:
www.elenaaitken.com
elena@elenaaitken.com